TO REAP A POMEGRANATE

A GREEK MYTH REIMAGING

LYDIA LYRE

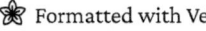

DEDICATION

To the women with more rage than they know what to do with.

DISCLAIMER

To Reap a Pomegranate is a dark fantasy romance that reimagines Persephone's myth, particularly her relationships with Hades, Thanatos, and other cthonic gods. It is meant for readers ages 18 or older. While inspired by Greek mythology with references to the original myths (particularly Orphic myth), this is entirely a work of fiction separate from the mythos.

Readers should be aware of the following content warnings:

- Death
- Murder
- Kidnapping
- Memory loss
- Mentions of suicide
- Mentions of past sexual assault
- Mentions of past domestic abuse
- Mentions of incest in the context of Greek gods
- Implied reference to an abortion, not had by the protagonist

This book also contains sexual content, including but not limited to voyeurism, cock warming, public acts, and exhibitionism. All sexual content between the protagonists is consensual.

PLAYLIST

- Pomegranate Seeds by Julian Moon
- Gold Dust Woman by Fleetwood Mac
- the fruits by Paris Paloma
- King by Florence + The Machine
- High Infidelity by Taylor Swift
- labour by Paris Paloma
- Persephone in the Garden by Aidoneus
- illicit affairs by Taylor Swift
- Guilty Pleasure by Chappell Roan
- last woman on earth by Paris Paloma
- Never Love an Anchor by The Crane Wives

PROLOGUE

SEPH

I've never had a worse migraine, but for now, I ignore it. My best friend shakes as I walk her up the steps to the clinic. It's so damn loud thanks to all the protestors across the street. Their screams drown out her sobs as tears streak down her cheeks. For all they know, we could just be here for Pap smears. But they all hold signs up with images meant to pluck heartstrings and stir guilt.

It is not what she needs to see right now. Not after the atrocities done to her.

And then, a woman yells, "It's all in god's plan!"

I seethe. What kind of god allows this to happen? What god thinks suffering is acceptable?

I think back to my studies, old hyperfixations and college courses. The Abrahamic god asked men to slaughter their innocent children as a fucked up sort of test. In Greek mythology, Zeus took women without a thought to their consent, often shifting form to wriggle his way into beds. The Japanese, Norse, and countless other cultures have trickster gods, too.

But where is the justice? Is there *any* justice in god's plan?

Perhaps it comes in death. Perhaps judgment strikes and

strikes hard, finally smiting those who got away with harm. Life is so precious. It's a shame that others would turn that into undue suffering.

Feeling feisty today, I shout back at her. "What else was, huh? School shootings? Terminally sick kids? The Holocaust?"

I half expect to be smote, struck by lightning or set aflame. All that happens is the woman shuts up. Most of the crowd does. I wrap my arm around my friend tighter, kiss her temple, and urge her inside.

And weeks later when I sit beside her in court, holding her hand from the pews, I see how there is no justice.

So I take it upon myself. I grew up on the farms, and know how to use all the equipment. I know how to tend to the soil. My mother preferred to harvest lavender with a scythe, and taught me proper techniques as a child.

The mountains hold secrets as old as time. They hold mine, too. How my pretty face was the last he saw before I bound him, having lured him like a siren. How my scythe ran across his skin, making a clean cut, leaving him to bleed out.

And how I felt nothing at all as I threw his body in his car and staged the accident.

The accident was deemed just that: an accident. His body was so blistered and burst that even the coroner didn't realize he died before the car rolled off, the weight of rigor mortis settling on the gas pedal enough to crash him into that pole. Enough alcohol in his system to deem him a drunk driver. No further investigation required.

No one ever caught me. Only the lavender and the mountains know, and the steel of my scythe.

I expect once again to be smote. But there is no lightning, nor spontaneous combustion or flames. No hellfire drags me down.

Years go by, and I move to the city for school under the guise of seeking a better education than my hometown can give. It's true enough for the excuse to work, and the more time passes, the more I am certain.

If there is a god, then they let it be known: if I want justice, I best serve it myself.

CHAPTER I

THANATOS

I rarely stay in the realm of mortals longer than I need to, but today, I make an exception. Humans call me by many names: The Grim Reaper, Death Personified, *La Muerte*, *Shinigami-sama*. After countless years, I've seen every inch of the earth's surface to hear them all. As such, I feel no need for sightseeing.

But I linger here, somewhere in what the mortals call the Pacific Northwest. Jobs like this one are my least favorite.

The sun beams overhead. I flip my black hood up to shield my eyes, now shrouding my face. Instant relief. No matter how many times I've visited the surface over the last few thousand years, I never grow used to its brightness.

My feet feel heavy as I drag them along the cobblestone streets. There's no avoiding death. I know that better than any, and yet I still dread what I must do today.

The death of one before their time is always such a tragedy.

When I'd received the assignment from Hades himself, I hadn't dared question it. Never did. The two of us hold a mutual respect for one another. I couldn't care less if the Lord of the

Dead likes me, and I simply tolerate the Master of the Palace. Both of us have a job to do. Those jobs aren't pretty, yet someone must do them.

For some souls, I carry my scythe, letting them know their time had come. But the moment I lay my eyes on Persephone Dumont, I let it return to the Underworld in a puff of dark smoke. Instead, I send my gentler companion, a black swallowtail butterfly, to her. Its wings flutter across the street, where Persephone sits outside a cafe. She's alone with a cup of tea and a book. My butterfly captures her attention when it lands on a page. When my swallowtail flies back, her gaze trails after it before her gaze lands on me.

I do not often pay much attention to the mortals I reap. A job is a job. They all must be delivered so Hermes can guide their souls below.

But as her eyes widen at the sight of me, I take note of her. Of the way the sun makes her dark hair look almost red. Her sand-colored skin, dotted with sun spots across her nose and cheeks. Her face looks so much like her namesake, the goddess's, that I do a double-take. And her eyes, blue as the sky, remind me of Zeus's. I'd only met the God of the Heavens a handful of times, but those piercing eyes were enough to remember him by.

Persephone Dumont is not meant to die yet.

And yet, she's been ordered for reaping today.

At least she'd pass on a beautiful afternoon. A rarity, from my understanding, of the times I've visited this part of the surface. The locals call it Seattle.

I teleport across the street, stepping in and out of shadow. She blinks at me as she sips her tea. From up close, now that I stand behind the chair opposite her, I see the resemblance to the Queen of the Underworld even more. It's unnerving.

Persephone looks around, then back at me, like she can't believe her eyes. Like I'm not supposed to be here—which would be an accurate assessment—and to confirm I'm here for her.

"You're Thanatos."

The way she says my name makes something tighten beneath my ribs. An unfamiliar feeling. It's been a long time since anyone's regarded me by my name, not my title.

"You know who I am. That should make this easier, then."

"I was really into Greek mythology growing up. My parents named me after Persephone, but everyone calls me Seph." She gazes at her thumbs as she twiddles them, as if aware she's rambling. "Is it my time already?"

It technically isn't, but for some reason, it's been overridden. All I say is, "I'm afraid so," because I don't know how to tell her Hades sent for her. Revealing that would open a can of worms I'm not prepared to answer, since I do not know why. So it's easier to just say yes, even though it's only a half-truth. Even though I wish I could explain to her how sorry I am.

Her voice drops to a whisper, focusing now on her tea. "Will it hurt?"

"No. Not with me, it won't." That, at least, is not a lie.

The ceramic of the teacup clatters as she sets it down, and the book in her other hand shakes. *She's* shaking. "Good. That's good, I suppose. No one wants a painful death."

"You'll feel no pain. I can ensure your comfort in your last moments. Normally, I reap the soul, then transfer to Hermes. He takes souls to Charon. But I'll be escorting you myself the whole way. Special orders."

Seph looks up at me again, eyes meeting mine. "Why? Did I do something bad?"

The urge to comfort her strikes me again, feeling so odd that it twists my gut. "I wouldn't know. Not my judgment. Though I suppose if you did, Ares would be here in my stead. He takes on those assignments."

But I can tell from her aura, from her demeanor, that she did nothing wrong. That she's a kind woman. And something about her is so familiar that it aches. I chalk it up to how much she reminds me of Persephone, whose absence for nearly 26 years is sorely noticed and missed. Even their names being the same strikes a chord within me, in a way not even Orpheus could.

Perhaps it's why I'm still talking to her. I typically don't say this much.

"May I at least finish my book? I only have a chapter left, and I'd hate to not know how it ends."

Death waits for no one. And yet I take the seat across from her. "I'm in a generous mood. Go ahead."

As the small relief washes over her, the smile on her face is genuine. I can see the muscles in her human form relax. "Thank you."

I'm glad I let her finish the book. Her jitters subside with every page turn, its contents giving her something to distract her nerves. As she reads, I study the cover so I don't spend the entire time ogling her. It's a romance novel, though not one I've heard of. The couple embracing on the cover might make others blush, but not much stirs my heart. Nothing or no one ever has.

Her tea sits half-full as she closes the book. With a deep sigh, she says, "Okay. I'm as ready as I'll ever be, I suppose."

I stand, then extend a hand to her. "My touch may be cold, but I swear to you that you'll feel no pain."

Seph takes my hand, and just like that, her soul splits from her body. As I take her below, I can't shake the familiarity between us. With the goddess gone, the name still snags in my chest like a jagged thorn.

Her name echoes in my mind, relentless.

Persephone.

The River Styx flows below us, black and infinite, lapping at the edge of the obsidian path. I don't make a sound as I walk, but her footsteps echo faintly. Curious. Most souls forget how to step by now.

She glances around, the edges of her form flickering. "Where are we going?"

I say nothing. The Palace is ahead, and that is answer enough.

The Palace of Hades rises before us like a mausoleum, and filled with equal amount of memory and grief. Its pillars stretch high into shadow, each etched with names long buried. Violet flame flickers in sconces carved into the stone, casting jagged shadows. Incense clings to the air, sharp, sweet, and bitter. Smells like home.

Souls drift through the grand entrance hall. Some moan, some mutter. A few sob. I lead her past them all. My special orders included delivering her directly to the Master himself. She watches the others as they pass—shades with no faces, no memories. She is still whole. Still awake.

"I didn't think it would feel like this," she murmurs.

"What did you think it would feel like?" I ask, surprising myself. I've never thought of what mortals might think.

"I thought I'd disappear. Which realm is this? Tartarus? Asphodel Meadows?" Seph asks. "You mentioned something about special orders?"

"They've given me no details, so don't ask follow-up questions." My tone is as flat as ever, not invoking fear or pleasure either way. "But yes, special orders. This is the Palace of Hades, where the Lord of the Underworld and the rest of us gods reside, alongside select shades here for work or punishment."

We pass the central corridor and make our way to the throne room. Shades wait in line for records to be drawn, names to be inked into the books of the dead, as they wait for Hades to hold court. The throne at the end of the hall is empty. I shouldn't be surprised that Hades would request an early reaping, only to not be present. He's never late for court, either.

My mother, Nyx, watches from near the wall, her eyes unreadable. Her gaze flicks from me to the soul beside me. She says nothing, but I feel her awareness press into me like mist through armor. Nyx must know what is going on, what's happening.

"Come," I say, guiding Seph to my mother. "No need for you to wait in this line. Mother," I call, and Nyx nods at me. Her black robes billow around her, contrasting against her long curls. Whereas my mother's skin is as dark as the night and her hair shines like the moon, I am the opposite, with dark waves and skin the color of starlight.

"My dear son. You've brought a guest. Lord Hades will return momentarily. He'll meet her outside." She hands me a small, golden key and raises a brow to ask if I understand.

I know what the key is for.

With a nod, I take the key from my mother, thank her, and lead Seph along.

I take her down the corridor. We pass the Lethe as I bring her toward the Garden of Pomegranates. It is not part of the original design. Persephone—the goddess—carved it into the bones of this place when she returned. A quiet place. A refuge, a reminder of spring.

Lord Hades locked the gates to the garden when Persephone died nearly thirty years ago.

The moment we step into it, the air changes. Green vines coil around marble. Lilies bloom from cracks in the stone. The torches burn golden after having been snuffed out for three decades. The air smells of citrus and myrrh.

She inhales, her form shimmering more solidly for a moment. "It's beautiful. Have you brought others here?"

"None."

I look away, but her presence lingers behind my eyes like sunlight on closed lids.

She walks among the flowers, touching nothing. Just seeing. The souls who end up here are few. Most don't remember enough of who they were. They fade or dissolve.

She doesn't.

And her name is *Persephone.*

The way she stands there—in this garden shaped by mercy and rebellion—strikes something within me. Something buried. Something I can't name.

I step back. "I should return to my duties. The Master will be with you shortly, I'm sure."

She smiles, faint and wondering. "Thank you for your kindness, Thanatos. Will I see you again?"

I should lie. I should say no.

But I don't.

"Perhaps."

With a smile, she turns back to the lilies. I walk away before I can say something foolish.

I teleport away, reaping as many souls as I can before I retire for the night.

The garden's scent lingers on me even now. My armor leans untouched against the far wall, and I haven't bothered to remove my gloves. I shouldn't be still. I never am. But here I sit, boots dusted with ash, scythe propped against the door, and I can't move.

Her name keeps echoing.

Persephone.

It's foolish. Dangerous, even. I've harvested thousands—no, tens of thousands. Mortals are fragile, forgettable things. Most

11

don't even get names worth remembering. Even fewer ask questions. Fewer still make it below with any clarity left.

But she did. And the garden bloomed upon her entry.

That unsettles me most of all.

This mortal Persephone, whoever she was, carried some quiet gravity. It reminded me of her, yes, but it wasn't mimicry. It was something else. Something gentler. Something unexpected.

I close my eyes.

In the stillness, I feel it again—that moment her soul separated, and the moment I first saw her before that. I knew her name before she spoke mine. That's part of my burden. Souls know me, and I know them. Not always by their deeds, but by what they've left behind.

Persephone.

She had no crown, no godhood. No throne of blooming vines or rebellion in her voice. She was just a woman. Mortal. Forgotten by the world, perhaps. Even if she had family who would miss her, they, too, would pass in time. But in death, something of her stayed sharp. Her soul didn't crumble upon arrival. She didn't recoil.

She followed me like she trusts me.

Gods, why does that matter?

I lean forward, elbows on my knees, gloved fingers laced. There's no time to be thinking about this. I have other souls to reap, other names to carry. And yet, I know that if I were called back to the surface and her face flickered before me again, I would feel that same strange catch in my chest. Not pain. Not longing. Just recognition.

It's absurd. Souls don't matter.

I remember the first time I met the real Persephone. The goddess. Before the chaos. She had looked at me like I was something she could never understand, but didn't fear. Despite the natural warmth about the Goddess of Spring, she held a sadness to her. She carried that with her until the day she died. The memory of her lingers, no matter how many seasons pass. How many years.

And now, this mortal. This namesake. This soul.

She asked if she'd see me again.

I should have walked away without looking back.

CHAPTER 2
SEPH

T he Garden of Pomegranates blooms beneath my feet. Other than the pomegranate trees, there are flowers sprouting from the earth, poplars, and myrtle trees intermingling with other citrus-bearing branches. Everything we passed on the way here fills me with dread, the darkness so all-encompassing I fear it may swallow me whole. But this garden feels special. It's odd how nothing decays here. Even in death, this place refuses to rot.

The garden feels familiar in a way nothing else does, save for Thanatos's presence. Not the courtyards, not the faceless procession of shades. Never in my wildest dreams did I imagine the myths I'd heard as a child would be real, nor would I have imagined Death Incarnate himself to be so beautiful. His skin is ghostly pale, a cool white tone that doesn't seem possible. It makes his chest-length black hair look like a shadow swirling around him.

"Will I see you again?"

I feel a tug toward him, strange as it seems. Something shimmers in his gaze, which highlights how much his eyes resemble opals: a pale blue, almost white, around the iris, with a rainbow of colors reflecting in them. It's stunning, albeit inhuman, though I shouldn't be surprised—he's a god, after all.

He's a god, and I'm here, in the Palace of Hades, wondering why. As far as I'm concerned, I'm no one special. I didn't live an extraordinary life. I'm the daughter of lavender farmers who went to school in the city. The shock of everything hasn't hit me yet, and I wonder if it'll ever sink in.

"Perhaps." Thanatos's lips twitch in the hint of a smile, and then he vanishes in a shroud of shadow. Already I miss his presence, aware of my loneliness in The Garden of Pomegranates.

I sit at a bench by the myrtle tree, fingers trailing through soft clover and cool violet petals. The air here is sweeter than I envisioned it would be in the land of the dead. I'm not sure how long I sit here for before the temperature drops. The weight of a presence settles behind me like a cold hand on my shoulder. I rise and turn toward the gate.

A tall figure stands at the edge of the garden path. Cloaked in deep black, his crown is made of jagged obsidian. Red eyes meet mine and for a moment, I forget how to breathe. I've never seen this man before, but my chest seizes—pain, recognition, fear, swarm all at once. Even though I don't know him, I know men like him. They carry themselves with the entitlement they feel to whatever they want.

He says nothing as he stares at me, as if looking at a secret he thought he'd buried. As if *I'm* what he wants and feels entitled to, even though I can't fathom why.

"Are you..." My voice is steadier than I feel, even as it trails off. "Are you the Lord of this place?" Because I can't bring myself to say his name. *Hades.*

His expression doesn't change. But the surrounding air thickens. His voice is low, like the rumbling of an earthquake. "I am." His eyes flicker with pain, maybe. Or memory. "We made this garden for you."

The words hit like a pebble dropped in a still pond. My stomach turns. "I don't understand."

"No. You wouldn't." He looks at me like he's seeing two people at once. One that I am. One that I'm not yet. Or was once before. "Do you believe in reincarnation?"

My phantom heart beats against my chest, as fast as a hummingbird's wings. Nausea overwhelms me, and I want nothing more than to run. But I've nowhere to go. I wouldn't even know where to run. And based on how damn tall he is, and how muscular—his black robes do nothing to hide his wide frame—if it came to a chase, he'd catch me.

Stroking his black beard, he steps closer. Not too close, but enough that I can see the fine lines around his eyes. The exhaustion behind them. "Answer my question."

"In reincarnation? I'm not sure. Though I suppose if I'm here, of all places, then anything is possible." I try to laugh off my nerves, but it comes out more like a strained exhale. "Did I have a past life?"

"You did. Here, in this palace."

"What was I to you?"

He doesn't answer right away. When he does, it's quiet. "You were everything."

My breath catches. I don't understand him right away, but when I do, it breaks my mind open like a thawed river. I shouldn't believe him, not as the wind stirs the myrtle tree. Petals fall between us like snow. Or perhaps that's exactly why I should believe the implication.

"Just because I was named after the goddess of spring doesn't mean I am her."

"No. It doesn't. But that's not why I know. You were my wife for millennia. Do not think I would not know your soul. At last, you've returned to me."

I go still. My breath—*can I even still breathe? Is that what this feeling is?*—sticks in my throat. My hands tremble at my sides, and I clench them to keep him from seeing it. I feel like a deer caught in the gaze of something old and patient and hungry.

"I don't know you," I say, my voice sharper than I mean it to be. "Don't talk to me like you do."

His eyes darken slightly, but he doesn't look angry. He looks hurt. That might be worse. Hurt men lash out, resulting in hurt women. Dead women.

"You knew me once. You knew this place. This garden. Me."

"No," I whisper. "I didn't."

"You were my wife," he says. The words land like a stone in my chest.

I step back—one, two paces, nearly tripping over a root that wasn't there before. My heel twists on the stone, and I catch myself against the bench, breath hitching.

He doesn't move. He watches me unravel, like this is something he's seen before. Like he's waiting it out.

"You're insane," I say, and there's a tremor in my voice I can't hide now. "I'm not *her*. I'm not anyone's anything."

He tilts his head. "You don't feel it? Not even here?"

"I feel like I'm about to be buried alive."

Something flashes in his eyes. Surprise, maybe. Regret. But it vanishes just as quickly.

"I waited decades for you to return to me," he says. "Your soul always finds its way back. It did every season, so it was only a matter of time before it did again. I only hoped I would be here to see it. And I am."

"Stop it!" I snap. "Don't talk like that! I'm not yours. I'm not anyone's."

After all, I am already dead. What is the worst that can happen?

He finally takes a step forward. I flinch so hard my back hits a stone bench. It doesn't even hurt; my body's too numb for that now, and I'm not sure if my new form can even feel pain to begin with.

"I will not hurt you," he says, slowly, like he's approaching a wounded animal. "You've been through a transition. You're disoriented. But this place, it's part of you. You'll remember. You'll feel it soon."

I shake my head. "You sound like a cult leader."

That stops him.

For the first time, the weight in his expression wavers.

I take the opportunity. I push off the bench and start walking—fast, erratic, one eye still on him. Every iota of my being, or whatever is left of it, screams danger. I can't get away from him soon enough.

"Stay away from me."

"Persephone—"

"Don't call me that!"

The name tears something open in me. Not a memory— nothing that clear. Just pain. Ancient, suffocating pain. And I don't even know why.

"You're mistaken," I say again, though my voice is cracking. "You've made a mistake. I'm not her. I'm not your wife."

I don't give him a chance to respond. I run.

The Garden of Pomegranates seems to bend around me, trying to trap me in loops of ivy and stone, but I keep going. I don't stop until I've put half the palace between us. Until the scent of myrtle fades and the cold sweat on my back dries. The corridors, too, warp as I go, leaving me disoriented and lost. I look for Cerberus, feeling the urge to snuggle up to something soft and fur-coated, even if it's a three-headed beast. If I'm the woman Hades says I am, then the dog will respond to me in kind. But there's no sign of him here, so I am denied even that comfort.

Only when I give up do I collapse into a dark hallway, pressing my back to the wall, chest heaving. He's wrong. He has to be wrong. Because if he's right, then I'm not just dead.

I am trapped.

I don't know how long I sit there. Based on how stiff my body becomes, it must be days, but time feels too still. I can't tell.

My breath saws in and out of me like a knife against bone. The corridor is dim and hollow, lit only by flickering torches that cast long, warping shadows across the walls. I try to shrink into the stone, like if I make myself small enough, I can disappear from this place entirely. From him.

Every sound feels too loud. Every footstep echo is a possible return of Hades, so I don't feel safe enough to leave.

My nails dig into my palms. I need to stay grounded. I need to not fall apart. But the panic keeps rising, thick and feral, curling around my ribs like vines.

Then I hear footsteps. Not just in passing, but soft, careful movement coming down my hidden little hallway.

I hold my breath.

"Persephone?"

I know that voice. It's Thanatos.

I exhale so hard it nearly breaks me in half. A sob escapes my throat before I can stop it.

"Hey, hey." He rushes forward. His voice isn't cold like Hades's. It's low and gentle and real. He kneels beside me, opal eyes scanning my face, concern etched into every line of him. "I've been looking for you. You weren't in the garden, and then… by the gods, what happened?"

I reach out without thinking and grip his arm. He's solid.

Grounding. Not a phantom in the dark. Not a voice calling me his wife.

"I didn't know where to go," I whisper. "I don't know my way around."

He doesn't pull away. He crouches beside me, steady and silent for a long moment, and then says, "Did someone hurt you?"

My voice shakes. "He said I was his bride. But that can't be possible, can it?"

Thanatos's eyes flicker. I don't know him well enough to read him yet, so I can't decipher it.

"Hades."

I nod. "I don't remember him. He already decided who I was. And I'm not... I'm not that person. There's no way."

"You don't owe him anything."

The words are such a relief I nearly cry. "Everyone down here talks like I'm supposed to know everything. I've heard whispers in passing, rumors based on my name alone. But I don't know, and I'm scared."

Thanatos hesitates, then sits beside me against the cool wall, letting the silence stretch between us until it becomes something softer than fear.

"I know how overwhelming the palace can be," he says eventually. "How it twists things. Even for us who've been here for... well, a long time. But you're not crazy. And you're not alone." He glances down the hall, then back at me, voice a little quieter. "And you don't have to go back to him."

I stare at him. "Won't he make me?"

"Perhaps," Thanatos says. There's no hesitation in it. "But he won't hurt you. I'll make sure of it."

I close my eyes, the tightness in my chest easing just enough to breathe.

"Thank you," I whisper. "I... I don't know you that well, either. But I trust you."

He says nothing to that. He doesn't have to. But he stays.

And for the first time since I arrived in this too-hot, echoing palace, I don't feel like prey. I feel safe, if only for a moment. Exhaustion sinks its claws into me, and Thanatos must notice because he offers, "Let me escort you to your chambers."

"I don't want anyone to see me."

"Then I'll teleport with you. Is that alright?"

"Are they shared with him?"

"No. They're yours and yours alone."

"Can you take me inside of them? So I don't need to be outside the door?"

Thanatos nods, touches my bicep, and then we vanish. In a blink, we are sitting on the edge of my bed.

"Get some sleep," he says. "While not a necessity any more, it will make you feel better."

With another poof, Thanatos is gone. I don't even get to ask him why he was looking for me. I can't dwell on it, either, because sleep takes its hold on me almost instantly, leaving me to drift in a dark river in my dreams.

In my dream, the river sends me back home. Within the lavender fields where I grew up, Thanatos waits for me. He's resplendent in his black robes, loose enough to reveal his chest and the muscles running along his side. He says nothing as I join him beneath the sun, which warms my skin with life, so different from the heat of the Underworld.

At first, the kiss of death feels metaphorical. There is no other explanation in my brain for why I dream of Thanatos kissing me, his lips as gentle as a butterfly's wings. The black swallowtail he sent after me flutters by, landing in my hair as he kisses me deeper.

But as our hands roam, I'm not so sure my dream is a

metaphor of my recent departure from the mortal realm. In my dream, my robes match Thanatos's. When I shift to touch his thigh, my breast spills out from the fabric, exposing it to the sun and to him. My nipple pebbles at his cold touch when he cups it, squeezes it, like I belong to him.

Like I belong to Death.

And with how gentle he is, I don't mind the thought.

CHAPTER 3
THANATOS

Word spreads fast through the Palace. Seph felt familiar because she was familiar.

Not a mortal after all.

Our Queen returned, but with no memory of her life before. To forget eons must be torture, and I can only think of her—her soft voice, her trepid gaze—over the next few days. How scared she was when I found her in that hallway, and how confused she must be.

And I, too, am confused. To silence my mind, I must sort out this mystery.

Megaera guards the archives, as bored as ever. "What can I do for you, Thanatos?"

My voice is flat, matching not only Megaera's tone but the one I use for most social interactions. "You can let me through."

As one of the snakes in her blonde hair assess me, she raises an eyebrow. "What do you need in the archives? Don't you have souls to handle?"

"My reapers are on it today."

When we first ruled, we had fewer souls to manage. Now,

with the explosion of populations, I've taken on some trust-worthy shades to help with the influx. This way, we can all get a break from time to time. I resisted rest for years, but now it is mandatory.

"And what brings you, of all people, into the archives?"

"Perhaps I'm in the mood for some light reading."

Megaera scoffs. "You *would* consider this light reading. Whatever, Thanatos. I trust you. Go on." She steps aside, opening the door for me to head in.

The door seals behind me with a low groan, swallowing the sounds of the Palace.

It's colder down here than most of the Underworld, which otherwise runs hot. The still air carries no scent, no life. Rows of shelves stretch into darkness, each one heavy with scrolls, ledgers, and memory. The ghost-lights drift above, flickering blue, barely enough to see by, but I don't need much.

As I pass through the shades punished to process paper-work for Hades, we all ignore one another. Exactly how I like it.

Each record here marks a life ended. Every soul Ares and I have touched has a page. Some are brief, others heavy with wars, betrayals, or traumas. I've never bothered to read most of them.

I head straight to the most recent files, alphabetically sorted thanks to the souls at work. Abusing my powers, I summon Seph's right to me so I don't need to search.

Persephone Dumont: twenty-five years old at the time of her death, but meant by the Fates to reach her mid-nineties. A clean record of a life, save for one murder, pardoned by Neme-sis. Ares reaped her victim, who appeared to be no victim at all. It's hard to fathom the sweet woman I met drinking tea and reading a book, soaking up the sun in a dress, as capable of murder, even if he deserved it. But as I read on, I can't help but smile when I see she killed him with a scythe those seven years ago.

Most importantly, her soul was, in fact, the reincarnation of our goddess, and Hades's request cost her seventy years of her life. While the palace celebrates her return to immortality, I remember the hollowness behind the Goddess of Spring's eyes, the gauntness in her cheeks. The depression. The misery and yearning to return to the surface.

I understand the special orders now. Hades wanted his bride back. Rather than waiting another seventy years—long for a mortal, but a blink for gods like us—he wanted her young and beautiful forever. The thought churns my stomach.

Not wanting anyone to see me, I teleport to the garden. It's not my place to check in on the dead. Once I deliver a soul to Hermes, it becomes someone else's burden. Charon's, the judges, Hades's. But I'm here, anyway.

Seph is here alone, tending to the pomegranates. Her spectral form has stabilized, so she looks alive again. Whole, like one of us. The haze that clung to her when she arrived has lifted, and now she wears her name as if it fits her. She's dressed like one of us now, in white robes that drape loosely on her frame, though the garment hugs her curves. Her lips are the color of pomegranate juice.

By the gods, Aphrodite must have blessed her.

As soon as the thought enters my mind, I shake it away. She's likely to be the Master of the Palace's bride once more.

I say nothing, opting to watch her for a moment. Seph is so engrossed in the trees, plucking the fruits from them, that she doesn't notice me. The trees are tall enough for her to reach, shorter than they would be on the surface. Made just for her.

When she turns to make her way to another tree, she spots me. She jumps a bit, then exhales. "Oh, Thanatos. I didn't hear you come in."

"My apologies. I didn't mean to startle you."

"You came back." Her voice is light, almost teasing. As though she always expected me to return.

"I was passing through," I lie.

"Of course." A knowing smile plays at her lips. "I'm glad you're here."

"That would be the first time I've heard that." I cross the grass, lush and soft beneath my boots, impossibly green for a place rooted in death.

"Did you know who I was when you reaped me?"

"No."

"Can you promise me something?"

"Depends. What can I do for you?"

"Everyone is talking to me like I'm the queen. I don't remember any of it, though. I don't even know if I really am the Persephone everyone wants me to be. The goddess, I mean."

"I read your file. You are. But whatever you need, let me know."

"Treat me as you would any other shade. Like you did when you reaped me. I need that normalcy."

I don't treat most shades the way I treated her. But she doesn't need to know that.

"What shall I call you, then?"

"Seph. Like when we first met."

"Seph. Of course."

She pauses, but I don't get the sense that she wants me to leave. I don't know what else to say, nor do I know why I came other than a strange desire to see her after learning the truth.

She asks, "Were we friends? Before, I mean."

"In your past life?"

Seph nods.

"We didn't interact much. But we were on good terms, I'd

say. My work keeps me busy, and kept me busier then. I have days off now, thanks to some hired help, but didn't always. In the few spare moments I had, if we were in a room together, we got along. You used to call me Than."

"Can I call you that now?"

"You may call me whatever you wish." She gives me a look, so I add, "Not because of your status. But because I've been called many names, and as such, do not care what you call me."

She smiles at that. "If I ask you about my past, will you tell me?"

"Assuming I know the answer, yes."

"Will you be honest? Or will you say what Hades wants me to hear?"

I swallow, sensing what she's getting at. "I've no reason to be dishonest. Nor do I care if what I have to say makes Hades happy."

"Even if Hades wishes otherwise?"

"While Hades may be the Lord of the Underworld, we are equals. We work in tandem. The only person I answer to as a superior is my mother Nyx, for whom this palace was built."

"You speak so formally."

"Do I?"

"Compared to what I'm used to. Maybe I'll adjust with time." She tosses a pomegranate in the air and catches it. "I suppose it doesn't matter if I eat the seeds this go-around."

Her words sink in. She's trapped here now, with no return to the surface. Before, Persephone would get six months above to visit her mother. But now, she's here permanently.

"No. It wouldn't matter."

"Do you like pomegranates?"

"I don't eat. No need to. Nor do you anymore, though some shades do still eat for pleasure."

Seph gapes at me. "Have you *ever* eaten?"

"Can't say I have."

She extends the fruit to me. "Would you like to?"

I stare at it. I've held scythes, blades, bones. By the darkness, I've held hearts in dying moments and kept my hand steady. But this?

If anyone else asked, I'd say no and vanish. But it's Persephone, trapped and alone, with no understanding of why. And perhaps it's because I take pity on her, but I take the pomegranate.

My glove brushes her palm. There's no warmth—of course there isn't. But there's a tether. A choice. This action may have consequences. If it does, I'll face them later. It's worth it to see the way her eyes light up at my acceptance, even though I'm not entirely sure why I care.

Using my thumb, I press into the fruit enough to open it, working the pulp as gently as I can. It's a clean cut, despite only being done by my hands, and I pass half of it to her. "Here. We can share."

She waits for me to eat the first seed. I start with only one, unsure of what to expect. A burst of flavor hits my tongue, sweet and tart all at once. It leaves a tang behind as I crunch it between my teeth.

"Do you like it?"

"It's pleasant."

"They're my favorite."

"They always were." With my free hand, I gesture to the garden. "You demanded he let you have this. Quite a rebellious spirit, you were."

Until the Underworld knocked it out of her. Until Hades drained it from her. Why he'd want a bird only to cage it, I'll never understand.

"Really?"

"You did. Said if Hades was going to force you to live here for half the year, you'd at least bring some life to this place. The garden only lives with your powers."

"If only it'd been so easy during my mortal life. Maybe I'd have killed fewer plants that way." She picks at some seeds, then says, "You know, it's funny. I grew up on a lavender farm with views of Mount Olympus. Not your Olympus in Greece. There's one in America, too, near the Pacific Ocean. A bit on the nose for a reincarnation, don't you think?"

"The soul likes what it likes, I suppose."

Her gaze lingers on me when I say that. I'm hyper-aware of the way she studies me, and I do the same to her. The curve of her nose, the freckles beneath her eyes. Features I normally would pay no mind to, I notice on her.

"How did I die? The first time, I mean."

"I'm not sure. None of us are. My brother Hypnos found you floating in the Lethe with an adamant dagger. Hades tortured the shades for years, but we never found out who did it."

She picks at her pomegranate seeds as we talk. "What became of the dagger?"

"Adamant is indestructible. Hades has the dagger locked up in his chambers."

She nods, a pensive look in her eyes. If she plans on stealing it, it won't be a simple task. None can enter Hades's chambers, though I suspect he may invite her in. Still, I doubt she'd be able to get in there alone.

"I'm surprised you're telling me this so freely."

"I've surprised myself." I offer her a small smile as I take another seed from my half of the pomegranate, enjoying the taste. "But my loyalty is to the Underworld at large, not one god. Hades would have none to rule over if not for me and Ares. We keep one another in check."

"And your mother, Nyx. Does she live here?"

"My father, Erebus, visits more than she does. Nyx has her own duties to attend to at the ends of existence. She came for your arrival, and makes time for my father when she can."

I've spoken too much, been here too long. I should leave, but I can't. My feet feel as if they're rooted to the ground alongside the pomegranate trees.

"And you? Are you here often?"

"I've reapers to help me attend to my duties. 'Often' is subjective." Her eyes drop when I say that, and it makes my heart sink to my stomach. This poor soul is looking for a friend, and has decided to find it in me. I cannot fathom why, but I also feel the urge to deny her nothing. It must be the pity I feel for her cut-short life, for the injustice of it all, that has me asking, "Is there anything I can do to aid in your comfort now that you're here?"

"It's lonely," she says. "I miss home. While I wasn't expecting your company today, it was welcome. So thank you, Than."

"I'll visit when I can." Because Seph needs a friend. Will need one more than anyone here if Hades is to pursue her how I suspect he will. And part of me feels protective over her in a way I've never felt towards any shade.

"I used to garden a lot, back on the surface. My apartment had a tiny balcony, so I had to get creative with it, but I enjoyed it. So if you're ever passing through again," her tone is almost teasing as she says 'passing through,' "then I'll probably be here. If you'd like to chat, or even be quiet."

"Noted."

She sits on a stone bench between some trees and pats the spot next to her with her free hand. "You can sit. Enjoy your pomegranate."

As she continues to pick at her seeds, their juices staining her fingertips, I hesitate. I've never sat with a soul. Gods, I hardly ever sit at all.

But I do. We eat our pomegranates in comfortable silence, and the whole moment feels as sweet and tart as the fruit itself. Lovely, but with that tang. It feels forbidden. I enjoy it anyway.

And for that very reason, the moment my half is empty of seeds, I teleport away, needing to vanish.

CHAPTER 4
SEPH

The Palace of Hades is easy enough to follow when the hallways don't twist to their own whims. Its great hall branches off to a few corridors, with one wing leading to the archives and Hades's office. The other wing leads to everyone's chambers, including mine. I spend most of my time in my garden, though there's also a lounge where many of the shades spend their off time.

I haven't seen Thanatos since we shared our pomegranate in the garden. My garden, apparently. His verification of my old identity was good enough for me to finally believe it. Coming to terms with it, though, is a whole other beast to tackle.

When I open the heavy gate to the garden again, Hades is already there. As if he knew I'd come. As if he's been waiting. Always waiting.

Hades says my name like it is fragile on his tongue. I tense, fingers curling into fists at my sides. No matter how brave I try to look, it doesn't match what's in my soul. I'm sure he can see right through me.

When I don't respond, his expression remains unreadable, carved from the same stone as the palace. He gestures to a small table I hadn't noticed before, now nestled among the myrtle branches. A tea service sits untouched on it. The cups are silver and dark porcelain, like someone tried to make it look inviting but didn't quite understand the concept of warmth if it wasn't from literal hellfire.

"I thought you might like a place to rest," he says. "Something familiar. You loved it here."

I can't fathom loving anything about this place. It's too dark, too devoid of life. My mind wanders to lavender, to mountains and pines by the water. "I don't remember loving anything here."

A breeze stirs the petals.

Still, he doesn't give up. "There was a time you'd sit under this tree and tell me stories of the mortal world. What the seasons tasted like. How spring smelled. You said I should try honeycomb sometime. I never did."

He says it with that same steady, sorrowful calm. As if the memory should soften me. As if it's meant to mean something.

It doesn't.

"You should stop," I gesture to the table, the tea. "Whatever this is. It's not going to work."

He tilts his head. "I only want you to be comfortable."

"No, you want me to remember." My voice hardens, remembering Thanatos's promise. He won't hurt me. "You want her back. Whoever she was. You don't care who I am now."

"I care deeply," he says, and for the first time, his voice is tight. Strained. He reaches up to one of the pomegranate trees, my pomegranate trees, and plucks a ripe fruit. When he rips into it, it makes a mess, its guts spilling down his pale fingers and wrists until they are stained red. "But it's true. I miss her. I miss you. Your laughter. Your defiance. Even your silent treatments."

As he eats a fistful of seeds, I flinch. "Then maybe you shouldn't have let her die."

He doesn't answer that. Good. I don't want to hear what excuse a god gives for grief.

Curiosity gets the better of me, though. I decide to twist the knife while I'm feeling bold. "Do you really believe everyone down here deserves to be here?"

His head tilts. Just slightly. "Pardon?"

"The souls," I say. "The ones moaning in the halls that you pass without looking at them. Are they all guilty?"

"I would hope so."

"But you don't know."

Shadows cling to his face. With his dark beard, it almost swallows all of his features except for those garnet-colored eyes. "There is a system. Judges. Laws older than Olympus. What would you suggest we do instead? Free them all on instinct?"

"No. But it doesn't feel like justice. It feels like routine. Like no one's thought to question it."

"Careful," he says, and it's not a threat—but it brushes the edge of one. Especially with how he's handled my fruit, taking from my garden without so much as asking.

"Why?" I ask. "Because I'm not supposed to question anything? Because I'm a guest?"

"Because you are still fragile," he says, voice booming so loud I feel it reverberate in my chest. "Whether or not you remember it, you are recovering from a wound that nearly unmade my world."

I blink. That catches me off guard. "What do you mean?"

He studies me again. "Nothing," he says. "Only that rebirth is delicate. It changes things."

We lapse into silence. I stare down at my hands. They still don't feel like mine.

He finally speaks again, quieter. "You were not always this curious."

"Maybe I should have been." I turn toward the path again. "This isn't some romance you get to revive with dead flowers and tea and wistful longing."

"Persephone—"

"I'm not her."

I don't wait for his reply. There's no point; the conversation is going nowhere, running in circles. I leave him standing under the tree, beside the tea set no one asked for, in the garden he built for a ghost.

As I pass wailing shades in line for Hades to address them at court, I ignore the way some of them reach for me, whispering names I don't recognize. Some call me *kore*. Some weep when they see my face. I keep walking.

I just need to find Thanatos. He's the only friendly face in this whole gods-forsaken place. He knows how to move through this palace, how to exist in it without becoming part of it. And when I'm near him, I feel something I don't anywhere else: a choice.

I check the atrium. The balcony where the stars look all wrong. The archives. The stone alcove where he'd once shown me how the souls are counted and recorded. His scent—cool air and cypress—is long gone.

I call his name softly once.

Nothing and no one answers.

I keep searching.

There's a lounge tucked near the kitchens, low-lit and velvet-draped. Hypnos, whom I've yet to formally meet but I recognize from the myths and his resemblance to Thanatos, sometimes naps there, but tonight it's empty. The hourglass beside the hearth has stopped. I touch it, wondering if time simply doesn't pass here.

Down another corridor. A guard nods at me but says nothing. A gorgon watches from a perch high above, her eyes glowing faintly. I don't ask her anything. I doubt she'd answer. Since I'm technically dead, I wonder if she could still turn me to stone. If she could, she might do me a favor. Spare me from this misery.

I find the chamber of records empty. The vaults, too. All stifling hot yet echoing.

No sign of him.

The emptiness grows louder.

I pause in front of a tall window that overlooks one of the deeper pits, bottomless and shimmering with a faint, otherworldly light. Somewhere down there, new souls are still arriving. Maybe he's working. Maybe he's avoiding me.

No. I won't think that. I can't think that he's avoiding me.

I press my forehead to the cold glass—thank the gods, it's cold to the touch—not sure how much longer I can bear this. Everyone here has some story they expect me to step back into. But when Thanatos looks at me, he doesn't expect a goddess. He looks at me like I'm just a girl who's trying to breathe.

I swallow hard.

Where are you?

I don't know what brings me to the sparring chambers. Maybe I think I'll find him here. Maybe I just need something solid—sweat and steel, a handle in my hands, the sound of bodies hitting the floor. Something real.

Red banners that curl like dried blood flank the stone archway. I pause beneath it. The scent of fire and old leather clings to the walls. My footsteps echo louder than I like.

There are three figures inside, all in motion. The tall one with the whip is unmistakable: Megaera. Her blonde ponytail coils behind her like a snake, and her stance radiates cold authority. After staring for a few moments, I realize snakes are, in fact, intermingled with her hair. Alecto hurls a jagged dagger at a training dummy, cackling when it explodes in a burst of ichor. And the third—Tisiphone—moves like a shadow. Silent. Eyes burning with madness and perfect focus.

They're beautiful and violent, and the air hums with electricity when they move.

I take a step back. Maybe this was a mistake.

Megaera sees me first. She turns, the whip relaxing in her hand, and raises an eyebrow. "Well, well."

Alecto's head whips around, the snakes in her hair along with her. "Oho. New girl!"

Tisiphone just tilts her head and stares, silent. Her snakes are as quiet and inquisitive as she is.

I freeze in place.

Megaera approaches slowly, whip now coiled at her hip. She studies me like I'm a puzzle. Or prey. Maybe both.

"I was wondering when we'd meet properly," she says. "Didn't expect you to wander into our little den of murder practice."

Alecto grins, sharp teeth on display. They're pointed, much like a shark's. "She's got balls if she's coming here. You know, given who she is and everything."

"I'm not," I mutter. "I'm not anything." Even though I am, I must be, for any of this to make sense. Perhaps if I can cling on to myself, to my past, my mortal life, I won't lose myself here. I can use it as an anchor.

Megaera hums. "Yeah. We've heard that one before."

They circle around me, not threatening, exactly, but curious. Feral. Their energy crackles against mine. I feel like a deer in the headlights of a storm chaser.

"I'm not here to fight. I was just..." I'm not sure how much I should tell them, "looking for someone."

Megaera folds her arms. "Thanatos?" When my eyes flick up

in surprise, she smirks. "I caught him snooping in your files when I was on guard duty at the archives. Since he never bothers me, I let him think I didn't notice. He had special orders to bring you here, yeah?"

"Leave her alone," Alecto says before I can answer. "Look at her. She's scared shitless."

"Not surprising," Tisiphone whispers. "Hades pressures."

They all nod at that like it's an inside joke. Like they, too, have been subject to it, and the only way to manage it is to laugh through the pain. Perhaps I could learn a thing or two from that.

"You don't have to be afraid of us," Megaera says, softer now. "Not unless you make it fun."

Tisiphone nudges Megaera with her elbow. "That's not helping."

Alecto snorts and throws an arm around my shoulder. I flinch, but she smells like ash and blood and lilac, and it's oddly comforting since it's so expected. "Relax, princess," she says. "We've got your back. Hades creeping around, trying to play husband to a woman who doesn't want him, huh? Welcome to the Greek pantheon."

A small laugh escapes me—a puff of sound, but genuine. It catches me off guard. The Furies all freeze for a second.

Then Megaera's smirk returns. "Okay, I think we can work with this."

"I'm just tired," I say honestly. "I'm not sure what you've heard. But I remember nothing before my mortal life. And it's so exhausting having everyone tell me who I'm supposed to be. Who I don't want to be, at that."

They go quiet. Even Alecto doesn't interrupt. Megaera steps forward and adjusts the collar of my cloak where it's gone crooked. It's a strange gesture—gentle. Almost sisterly.

"You're not the only one who had to become something they didn't want to be," she says. "We were chosen, too. Forged in blood and divine vengeance, or whatever poetic bullshit they dressed it up with."

"Don't worry," Alecto adds. "You're allowed to not know who you are here. That's practically tradition."

Tisiphone reaches out and brushes her fingers along my hair. "New life. New skin. We remember what that's like."

I blink fast. My throat tightens. "I still don't know if I belong here."

"You don't," Megaera says. Not rude, but matter-of-fact. "None of us do. That's the point. Come on. Sit with us. Let's get to know each other."

We sit on the cool stone of the chamber floor, passing a dented flask of something strong between us. Megaera—Meg, as she prefers to be called—tells me it's nectar she confiscated off a shade who snuck some in, a gift from the Olympian they worship. There's a saccharine sweetness to the drink, but it's wonderful and floral and fruity. According to Meg, it tastes different to everyone who drinks it. For me, it reminds me of my favorite teas. For the Furies, the taste is more metallic.

"Say, I've been meaning to ask someone. Where's Cerberus?"

Alecto answers. "He guards the gates at all times. Since you came in on Hades's order or whatever, I imagine Thanatos took you a different way, so you wouldn't have seen him."

After we drink, Alecto teaches me how to throw a knife without slicing off my own ear. To thank her, I show her how to use a scythe, a tool I haven't picked up since that fateful night. It's been enough time now that feeling the handle in my grip doesn't take me back to it all. When I tell them about my strange dream where I floated in the river, Tisiphone hums strange lullabies that she says will help me sleep. Megaera doesn't say much, but I feel her eyes on me, watching—not judging, but witnessing.

They don't ask more about Hades. And for the first time, I don't feel like a broken reflection of someone else's goddess. I just feel like Persephone, whoever that ends up being.

I hum the lullaby Tisiphone taught me that night, hoping it will help me sleep. While I find it faster, the dreams still come. Though, to Tisiphone's credit, they're clearer now than they were in the past nights.

I recognize the river I float along now, face-down in its water. As I drift, I lap at the water, drinking as much as I can. My throat is dry, no matter how much I swallow. The water is tasteless except for iron, and it soaks every inch of me. Robes stick to my skin, hair clings to my face, and I can feel it down to my bones. Lethean water reeks of rotten fruit, but I cannot stop drinking.

The iron flavor, I realize, is my blood as my hand drifts to the adamant knife sticking in my chest. I grip the hilt and pull it from my body, looking up from the dark waters only to observe the weapon. The stone handle holds a pale garnet, and the curved blade drips with my blood.

I'm out of my body, my soul shifting through the palace. Hades stands in the grand corridor, holding the still-bloody dagger to his chest as he declares the death of the Queen of the Underworld.

"Persephone stabbed herself and then jumped into the River Lethe."

Did I do that?

All I can feel is the way the Lethe does nothing to wet my throat, but plenty to empty my head, leaving a static fuzz between my ears. In my dream, I drink, and I drink, and I drink until I forget why I'm drinking.

CHAPTER 5
THANATOS

The summons comes without fanfare. Hades does not need ceremony when he wants something. His will carries like a weight through the halls of the palace, heavy and inevitable. I feel it before I hear it, as I always do.

As always, Hades's office is quiet. Low-lit, grand, and suffocatingly hot, like the rest of this place. It's filled with black stone columns, iron-braced bookshelves, and a desk chair that might as well be a second throne. Everything about it, like Hades, is carved to intimidate.

When I arrive, I don't expect to see Seph there. I stand next to her before Hades's desk, and it breaks my heart to see her like this. She's so different from the woman I first found at the cafe on the surface, and later in the garden those nights ago. When she's around him, Seph transforms.

She looks like she's trying not to be seen, barely lifting her chin. Her shoulders are drawn tight, and though her feet carry her forward, her hands twist nervously at her sides—fingers fidgeting, thumb tucked into her palm like she's trying to disappear into herself. Her gaze doesn't meet mine, or his.

"She looks well," Hades says, not to her but to me. As if she's not in the room. Even though, with the bags beneath her eyes and her bottom lip between her teeth, she looks anything but well. "Stronger. That's good. You'll need it."

She doesn't ask what he means. I don't think she wants to know.

I watch her carefully. Quiet observation is the only thing I allow myself. Every tilt of her body speaks. She stands as far from his desk as Hades will allow. She doesn't flinch when he speaks, but there's tension in her spine, the kind born of fear that's been worn into the muscle. I've seen that stiffness enough times on frightened mortals to know it when I see it.

"There's unrest in the lower realms," Hades says, voice clipped. "Petty grievances. Minor, yes, but the balance is delicate. Tartarus does not tolerate disorder."

I nod. "I've noticed the fluctuations. Sentence backlogs. A few misplaced spirits."

"Fluctuations." Hades laughs, low, no humor in the sound. "Is that what you call it when damned souls start arguing with judges about innocence?"

I say nothing as Seph shifts beside me. Her eyes are wide, darting between the floor and the walls—anywhere but his face. But that comment, that dig, was meant for me. I don't dare drop Hades's gaze, don't dare back down. One thing I learned a long time ago was to never show weakness.

Hades holds my gaze, then turns to Seph. I hate the way he looks at her like she's a piece of meat, even though I'm still not sure what drives my possessiveness. I've known of the injustices of our order for a long time, and I've done a good job paying it no mind until now.

Hades says to her, "You've asked questions before, about the palace. About judgment and justice." She stiffens, even though I didn't think someone could get stiffer. I wasn't privy to those conversations, but I'm intrigued. He continues with his voice as smooth as polished onyx, "Then go see how it works. Thanatos will escort you into Tartarus. Consider it an education."

Her voice is as meek as her posture when she finally speaks. "And if I don't want to go?"

He smiles. "Then you'll never learn anything useful."

Her breath catches, a barely audible sound. I feel it more than hear it, like a thread pulled taut.

"She'll be safe," I say. I'm not sure why I say it. Or if I believe it. But I do.

Hades leans back in his chair, satisfied. "Of course she will. Who better to protect her than Death himself?"

I don't answer. She looks at me now, finally, and I see a pleading in her eyes. She thinks I can protect her. I've even promised her such things. In truth, though, I don't know if I can. From Tartarus? Of course. But from Hades, I'm not sure. Regardless, I nod, and she follows me out of the chamber like a ghost chasing the one thing that might tether her to the world.

I keep my distance as we descend into Tartarus. She walks beside me, close enough that I feel her warmth, no longer mortal but now divine. She says nothing at first. I pretend not to notice her glancing at me. I'm good at silence. Silence is easier than the answers I don't want to give.

Tartarus greets us with the usual dirge: chains clinking, spirits muttering, fire groaning from beneath the stone. I know every step of this route. I walk it almost daily. Souls cry out as their punishments are carried out. Some deserve it. Others, I'm not so sure.

We stop at the sight of unrest, a platform meant for sentencing. There's a human woman, close in age to Seph. Seph stops to watch as the vrykolakas descend on her. The vampire-like creatures here are often sent to scare away dissenters, but the woman swats away at them, despite the shackles around her wrists.

Seph asks me, "Do you know her?"

"Ares reaped her."

The woman spits at one of the vrykolakas. "We don't deserve this!" As we get a closer look, I see other shades, mostly women, fighting against the creatures holding them back. They flash their fangs, but the women bare their teeth in response, unafraid.

"Do you know why?"

"Murder."

"Who'd she kill?"

Seph's question makes me realize I don't know this woman, not at all. I've made the same mistake as everyone else in this damned palace: thinking I know her, all because I once did. Seph may be our goddess reincarnated, but she's lived her own life. Had her own experiences, including murder—though I don't know why, only that Nemesis pardoned it because the man was vile.

Seeing this unfurl will tell me everything I need to know about Seph, though. Especially how she reacts to it.

"Well, this is the disturbance I'm meant to clean up. Ask her."

Seph is quiet as the vrykolakas lead us through Tartarus, but I feel her emotions the way I feel shifts in the veil between life and death. She's not afraid, but I can't name what she's feeling. It almost feels like anger.

We follow the vrykolakas through narrow passageways, down into a lower vault where the glowing chains of Tartarus pulse like veins. The vampiric guards have been pushed back. Shades of the damned swirl in chaos, but it's organized. Tactical. Ares would be proud.

Then we see the barricade of overturned iron benches. Chains have been cut and slung like whips. Standing atop it is a tall spirit with eyes full of wrath. She's surrounded by dozens of women, maybe more. Some are wrapped in scraps, some blood-ied, all of them confident in a way that surprises me. Their rage is their armor. Their defiance is their weapon.

I summon my scythe. "Stand down. Now."

The leader glares at me. "Death speaks. Finally."

Another woman spits on the ground. "We were judged by men who never heard our side. By rules written to protect the powerful."

"They called it murder," says a third. "We call it self-defense."

Seph steps closer. Her voice is soft, but clear. "What happened to you?"

The tall one looks at her, and the hard line of her jaw falters. "They sent us here because we wouldn't die quietly. We killed husbands who broke our bones and bruised our children, and said we should be grateful for it."

Another soul speaks up. "I slit his throat while he slept. I'd do it again. They call that damnation."

A murmur of agreement runs through the group.

My grip on my scythe tightens in uncertainty. The women will likely take it for a threat.

These souls are violent. They broke laws. Took lives. But I've seen monsters who walk free. And I've seen the judgment chamber shrug at cruelty if the name of the offender carries enough weight.

"They were never going to give us mercy," says one. "So we took it ourselves."

Seph turns to me. Her eyes search mine. "Can we do some-thing for them?"

My stomach twists. There is no protocol for this. These souls were condemned. Officially. Legally. But justice?

I look back to the barricade of women. Some are crying. Some clutch makeshift weapons. Not a single one looks repentant. And yet, I've never seen a group more certain of their righteousness.

Seph insists, "They're not evil."

"They still killed."

"Maybe. If you ask me, they were saving themselves."

The words hang between us.

And because I hate the way she's looking at me, I say something I've never said before.

"We can move them."

Her eyes widen.

"There are forgotten tiers," I explain. "Quarantine chambers for undecided cases. The judges won't like it, but I can make it happen. Just this once. But you'll need to exercise your authority."

Seph exhales like she's been holding her breath for days. "Will they be safe?"

"They'll be watched. But not tormented."

"Then do it. Help them."

I step forward again and raise my scythe toward the spirit leader. "You have two choices. Go back to your chains and rot, or come with me by order of the Queen."

The tall one hesitates before she assents.

It takes time to organize them. Seph speaks with many of them, listens, comforts, learns their names. I don't interrupt. She's doing what no one else has ever done for them: treating them like people. Not criminals. Not liabilities. As fellow humans.

Later, as I lead them to the hidden passage, Seph walks beside me again.

"You could've stopped them," she says. "You could've struck them down."

"But I didn't."

"Why?"

I notice her hands are smudged with ash from touching their broken chains. Then, I spot the worry still etched in her brow.

"I wanted to see what you would do."

We reach the sealed threshold: a backdoor, carved into the ribs of the palace, rarely used. As it creaks open, I glance back at Seph once more. Her light shines in the dark here. Not like the sun, but like a lantern held by someone who refuses to be lost.

"You were right," I say.

She raises an eyebrow. "About what?"

"This isn't justice."

Then I usher the women through.

When we're alone and returning to the palace, Seph reaches out, and I flinch before I can stop myself. It's only a simple, grounding touch, yet it breaks something in me. Some dam bursts as I look at her, and I've been wanting it to break for gods only knows how long. She's watching me the way mortals watch the stars they can't name. Like I'm far away, but not unreachable.

"For the record, I don't think you're wrong," I say quietly, not wanting to risk any other shades hearing. "About any of this."

Her brows lift in surprise.

"Then why do you let it happen?"

For the first time in my very long life, I put words to my feelings. "Because I have to keep moving. If I stop, if I feel it all, I'll drown."

She says nothing. Just holds my gaze. And in that moment, it's too much. I pull my hand away, as gently as I can so she doesn't take it the wrong way. But the warmth of her lingers.

The palace sleeps lightly at this hour.

The halls dim. Servant shades drift by wordlessly. It's late, but time doesn't hold its shape here, not in the Underworld. We're always either too early or too late.

I find myself on the balcony. My favorite spot to come after Tartarus missions.

It overlooks the Cocytus, the river of lamentation. Souls don't pass this way often. Even they know better. The air is thinner here, cooler and quiet. It's the only place in the palace where I can still hear my own thoughts without them echoing back too loud.

I don't expect her to follow me, but she does.

Her footsteps are soft, but not hesitant. She's learning how to move through the twisty halls, how to inhabit herself again. I glance back, and there she is: the reincarnated goddess named after death and spring, looking every bit like her namesake and like she doesn't belong here and never has. Selfishly, I can't help but be drawn toward her warmth, her brightness, like a sun pulling me in to her orbit.

Seph joins me at the ledge. Says nothing. We both stare out over the mist-draped expanse.

"You found this place quickly." My voice comes out lower than I mean it to. "Most don't find it at all."

"I looked for you," she replies, as if it's the most natural thing in the world to look for me. Most do not seek out Death Incarnate. Most run the other way.

I pause. "Why?"

"You left without saying anything once we got back."

"I tend to do that."

She huffs something like a laugh. "You don't say."

The silence stretches again, but it's not uncomfortable now. More like the stillness or pause between a heartbeat and a breath.

"I used to come here all the time," I say finally, surprised by the words. "Long before anyone knew my name. Before I had a task. Before I wore this cloak."

"Why?"

"Because this part of the palace didn't expect anything of me."

She rests her arms along the railing, hair brushing her shoulders. "I wish I understood that. Not having the palace expect anything of you, that is."

"It's watching you," I warn.

Her head turns. "Hades?" When I nod, she shivers. Whether from fear or the chill, I can't tell. I look away from her and down at the river below. "Do you want to talk about what you saw today? I imagine that wasn't easy for you."

Her voice comes after a long breath. "It wasn't right. Those women. They didn't deserve to be sent there."

"No."

"And the judges knew it. They just did it anyway."

"They did."

Seph faces me. Her eyes are lit with something raw—confusion, anger, sorrow all tangled together. "How do you stand it?"

My throat tightens.

"I don't," I say. "That's why I try to ignore it."

She's quiet. Waiting.

"When I began reaping souls, I believed it mattered," I continue. "That the order of things had purpose. That the darker parts of this were part of balance, even if I delivered souls here without pain. But I see how many fall through the cracks. How many are conveniently condemned, even the ones reaped by me rather than Ares. And still I go on, because if I don't, someone else will. Gods forbid Ares carry out my work, rather than just the violent and cruel."

Seph nods. "That's not justice."

"No. It's duty."

She looks at me like I'm someone else. Not Death Incarnate, not Hades's enforcer, not a god, but something smaller.

It should scare me.

It doesn't.

She shifts closer, not enough for the touch to be deliberate but for her warmth to reach me anyways. "I want to fix it," she says. And though her voice is soft, the conviction in it makes my breath catch.

I look down at our hands, resting side by side on the stone ledge. Hers is still trembling slightly. She doesn't hide it. Around me, she doesn't have to. I'm glad that, at least amidst all the madness, she feels safe enough to be herself around me.

I reach out without thinking. Our fingers brush, and the contact jolts through me like a sudden spring thaw. She doesn't pull away.

"Be careful."

Her lips twitch into a smile. "Why?"

"Because if Hades thinks you want to change something, he'll crush that dream before you have the chance."

She turns her hand over, palm up. I don't take it, not yet. First, I look at the lines there—delicate, unfinished, human. Only after I've examined them do I accept the offering. Her hand is so soft, so small in my own that a surge of protectiveness sweeps over me.

"And what about you?" she asks. "Will you try to stop me, too?"

I raise my gaze to meet hers. The darkness reflects in her eyes, turning that piercing blue into a stormy sea. The word leaves me before I can take them back. "No." But I don't want to take it back.

For once, I don't want to retreat into the safety of silence. Her fingers curl slightly toward mine. Not a command. An invitation. I let the moment hold, then step away before I can fall into it. She doesn't look disappointed, only understanding. The wind stirs around us, carrying with it the scent of wet stone and roses.

"I'll walk you to your chambers," I offer.

She nods, and falls into step beside me, our arms almost but not quite touching all the way back to her wing. We walk in silence, but it's not uncomfortable. If anything, it's a reassurance.

Seph still holds her resilience from her past, her rebellious nature. Except now, unlike the Persephone of old, she's not hiding it. She's not appeasing Hades. She's fueled with a rage that I don't think anyone can tame. And I fear, with what I've done by helping those women, that I've brought the fire stoker.

CHAPTER 6
SEPH

When I was in college, I studied abroad. First, in Rome, then in Athens. The irony of it all, now. While in Rome, visiting The Galleria Borghese, one piece of art in particular struck me. I stood before Ratto di Proserpina for so long, one of the museum employees came over to talk about it with me.

"The name is misleading, you see," she'd explained. "Rape then meant more of a seizure or abduction than the way we use it today. Persephone's willingness to live in the Underworld is still a heated topic among scholars."

Her words hung thick in the air as I stared at that statue, and I couldn't help but think it didn't seem much different than today's meaning. That there could hardly be any willingness in the way Persephone leaned away from Hades's grasp, despite the way his fingers dug into her ribs and thigh. No consent in the way she pushed away his face with one hand, reaching for the sky with the other as her face distorted in what looked like agony or a plea for help. If you look close enough, you can even see a tear halfway down her cheek.

Now, as the memories from my life before rush back in my

dreams, I cannot help but think of that statue once more. Of how the reality is so much worse.

My dreams show the myths once again, as if I'm living it. The sun shines on my skin, warming me as I gather flowers with other maidens. As I lean down to pick a poppy, the earth splits beside me. Riding a dark chariot, Hades leaps from the ground. Before I can run, the black horses trample down the flowers around me. Hades himself snatches me as I scream, the maidens taking chase as I am dragged below. I wriggle and squirm and kick, but nothing matters. Hades is too large, too strong, and forces me against his side. It doesn't stop me from fighting all the way down, even off the chariot, thrashing until he finally releases me in the throne room.

I move to run, but he grips my arm. "At least listen to what I have to say."

"Why would I do such a thing?"

"I don't want to hurt you. I wish to make you Queen, damn it."

"Let me go."

"Your father gave his blessing. What is done is done. I am alone down here, so you are to be my bride."

"Your loneliness is not my responsibility."

"It is now."

But I protest, refusing to leave my chambers, even to so much as eat. I miss my mother, her radiant smile and warm embrace. Yet now, thanks to some whim of my father to appease his brother, I may never see her again.

I don't know how much time passes until I am told I will get to return. That my husband must return me to the surface where I belong, lest my mother's own act of protest slaughter all of humanity above.

"My bride," Hades says, "you cannot return to the surface without any energy. Here. Eat these."

He hands me six pomegranate seeds, all resting in his palm.

"I told you, I don't want your food."

"You need it. To return above. If you want to see your mother again, you need the energy."

And in my desperation, I believe him. In my desperation, I eat the pomegranate seeds, damning myself to return.

In a cold sweat, I jolt awake from the dream as soon as I swallow the sixth seed, only to find a woman at the foot of my bed. We both yelp in surprise at the sight of one another. We look alike, with the same facial features, though her hair is split into two colors: one half like the night, the other whiter than milk. This woman's skin, too, splits similarly, half white and half black, matching her hair perfectly. Her eyes are like black voids littered with stars, little galaxies within themselves. She dons a saffron-colored robe.

I lower my voice. Similar to Thanatos, there's something familiar about her, a fragmented memory from my past that tells me I can trust her. "Who are you? What are you doing in my room?"

"Melinoë. You used to call me Mel. I'm your daughter. Well, was."

"Goddess of nightmares."

"That I am. I'm sorry if your recent visions have disturbed you. I swear, Mother, I'm only trying to help."

It feels strange, to have never given birth yet to have this woman call me Mother. "Can you call me Seph, please?"

"Sure. Seph." Melinoë tries my name a few more times, then says, "Odd, but I'll adjust. This must be so strange for you. I can explain."

"I'm listening." I sit up, curling the blanket around myself for comfort more than warmth. "You can sit."

Melinoë sits on the edge of the bed beside me, but keeps a healthy distance between us. I can tell she's doing her best to not frighten me. "They aren't dreams. They're your memories. I'm trying to send them to you the only way I know how. Are you alright?"

I'm not, not in the slightest. Part of me doesn't want to dump that on her, so I opt for a simple enough truth: "I'm homesick."

The way I yearn for home is unparalleled. From the lavender fields of my childhood to the city by the Puget Sound, and all the mountains surrounding them, I miss it. Now, I am stuck here, and I feel as if my skin is going to melt off from the heat, and—

Before I can have a full-blown panic attack, Melinoë snaps me out of my thoughts. "I'll talk to Hypnos. We can break up the visions. He can help you dream of home."

"That would be very kind of you. And don't worry, I do appreciate the visions, as awful as they are."

"You deserve to know who you're dealing with. The way Father looks at you..." Melinoë exhales as she chooses her words. "He's a master at manipulating people. I don't want you to fall for it. Not again."

"So how do you have my memories?"

"They're more so mine, or other people's who were there. I can't pull upon yours since they're lost to the Lethe. I won't deny my bias, though."

"That's good enough for me. You're trying to protect me. I can't fault you for that."

"I'm glad you see it as I do."

"Besides, I've no interest in Lord Hades."

"No? Has someone else caught your eye?"

"That's got nothing to do with it. I know the myths. They line up with what you're showing me, and I don't like what I see."

Though I'd be lying if I denied my attraction to Thanatos.

Like all the gods I've met thus far, Thanatos is a vision to behold. Power radiates off him, but it's not intimidating, at least not to me. Whereas Hades uses his darkness to incite fear, Thanatos's shadows feel like a warm summer's night. He may be death come to life, but there's a gentleness to him that makes me feel safe.

Melinoë, too, feels safe. While the Furies teach me about weaponry when they can, I don't yet know what to make of them. The idea of trying to make some sort of positive change flutters around my mind, but I can't do that without people I can trust. Melinoë makes for at least two, though I hope I can count the Furies in.

Melinoë says, "I can't stay long. I don't want him to detect my presence. But I'm glad we met. Truly."

"Likewise. Where can I find you during the day?"

"Attending to my duties. Wait for me at night. It's safer than you wandering."

It seems like nearly everyone here has the ability to puff away, and it makes me a bit jealous when she vanishes.

CHAPTER 7
SEPH

After Melinoë leaves, I struggle to find sleep. Putting on a robe, I slip out, making my way to the garden. A walk and some fresh air, no matter how hot it is, might do me some good. Being around plants always helps clear my mind, too.

The palace is eerily quiet. Even the shades drift like they're in a trance, avoiding my eyes, slipping past with the deference of fear or confusion—I can't tell which.

I turn a corner.

And there he is: Hades. Lord of the Dead. My captor. My— *no.* I stop the thought before it finishes. I am no longer his wife. This life is mine, not the old goddess's.

He's standing beside one of the tall obsidian pillars, speaking to a cloaked shade. His voice is low, too quiet to catch, but the finality in it is unmistakable. The shade bows so deeply its nose touches the ground, then retreats without a sound.

And then we're alone.

His head turns toward me before I can turn back.

Too late.

"Persephone," he says, in that voice like cracked stone and smoke, gentle in a way that makes my skin crawl.

I stop walking. My spine straightens on instinct.

"Hades," I reply, and the name tastes bitter.

He studies me with those strange, dark red eyes—too sharp, too still, hollowed and burning. For a moment, I wonder if this is the face I loved once, long ago. Or if love was something I only forced myself into for safety.

"You walk the halls freely now," he says, stepping closer. I don't think he means to be threatening, but it feels overt.

"Yes," I answer. "You said I could."

His mouth lifts at one corner. "So I did."

Hades takes another step. I can feel the cold before him—he doesn't radiate a chill, not like others do. The air around him always feels starved of life, like it's been suffocated by humidity.

I keep my voice as level as I can. "Did you want something?"

"Only to see how you're adjusting," he says. "The House is... vast. Difficult, even for those who remember it."

"I manage," I say, more firmly than I expect.

His eyes flicker, curious. "You're stronger now than when you arrived. You've put on some muscle." He tilts his head slightly, birdlike. "And are you starting to remember?"

I flinch before I can stop myself. His expression darkens just a little—not angry, but deeply, almost imperceptibly disappointed.

"No. I'm not." It's a lie I hope he doesn't catch.

"It will come. You are still you, Persephone. Even if the threads are tangled. You will find your way back."

I shake my head. "You keep saying that. But what if I don't want to?"

He's quiet for a long, heavy moment.

Then: "You did once."

"Maybe I didn't know better."

The words leave my mouth before I think them through. A sharp breath rushes into the space between us.

"Do not mistake fear for wisdom."

I narrow my eyes. "And don't mistake silence for consent."

There's the flicker of a flame in his eyes—fury? Hurt? I don't know. In a blink, he tucks it away behind a calm smile.

"You're spirited tonight," he says.

"I'm tired of being afraid."

Another pause. The silence between us is no longer empty, it's pressurized.

He softens his voice. "You will remember what we were, Persephone. What we are." He caresses my cheek, making me wince, but I'm frozen in place. Right now, I'm all bark and no bite against him. "And when you do, this will feel like home again."

He turns and vanishes into shadow before I can reply. I'm left in the hall with only my breath and the bitter taste of adrenaline rising in my throat. I don't remember what we were, but I know what we aren't.

My hands still shake when I reach the garden gates. And that's when I see Thanatos, the sight of him enough to have me releasing a breath of relief. The sound catches his attention, and he turns, saying only my name.

Not the full name. "Seph." The nickname I prefer, a prayer on his lips.

"Than. It's good to see you."

"Likewise. Are you busy? I find myself with some free time and a craving for pomegranate."

I can't help my smile. "Come on. Let's catch up."

As we enter and pick our fruit, Thanatos asks me of my life before: what it was like, the things I enjoyed the most, what I miss. My eyes well up as I tell him stories of my loved ones, my friends, my favorite hikes and ski slopes. I don't notice the first tear fall until Thanatos is beside me in a flash, wiping it from my cheek with his thumb. He's nearly frozen to the touch, but down here, it's a welcome relief. It makes me yearn for his hands, his whole body, to encompass mine. The thought alone gets me wondering how he'd feel beneath my robes, and no matter how hard I try to brush the thought away, it sticks.

"I'm sorry. I didn't mean to upset you."

Thanatos is so close, I can feel his cool breath on my face. He smells of lavender and spearmint, fresh and reminding me so much of home it nearly transports me back to the fields.

"I'm not upset," I reassure him. "These are happy tears. Sorry for worrying you."

"You've nothing to apologize for. Though, perhaps I do. I keep teleporting off on you. I'm sorry. I'm bad at... well, this. Talking to people."

"You told me once that if you stop and feel it all, you'll drown. I get that. Your role must come with a massive burden."

To be the one to deliver millions upon millions of souls to their death... I can't fathom the pain that must cause. How much easier it must be to keep everyone at an arm's length.

"It does. But it's one I'm willing to bear. One I'm good at bearing, or so I'd like to think."

"You are. You made this as easy for me as you could, you know. I'll never forget that kindness you showed me. How you let me read that last chapter."

To my delight, he smiles. It's so beautiful when his face lights up, a rare sight that I feel privileged to see. "I still don't know what compelled me to do that." When his eyes meet mine, I feel something within me snap into place like a magnet. "You must have caught me on a good day. Twice, now. That's a record."

"You did something good," I say, keeping my voice soft. "Whatever Hades says, know that we made the right choice."

"I'm not used to second-guessing myself. But I keep hearing their voices. The ones who fought back. The women who didn't get a chance to explain."

I glance at him. His face is calm, too calm, but there's a crease between his brows that wasn't there before. I want to reach out. But I don't, unsure of how comfortable he'd feel. We'd held hands earlier, sure. But I'm not sure if that was a fluke.

"They were just people," I whisper. "People no one listened to."

He exhales through his nose. "I listened."

I smile. "Because of me?"

He doesn't answer. Just looks at me. A slow, deliberate glance that lingers a moment too long. I feel it settle over me like a touch that doesn't quite land. It makes my chest tighten.

"Because something didn't feel right," he says at last. "And you see things differently."

"Maybe that's why I was sent back. Not to remember who I was, but to see what everyone else forgot."

Silence again. Not uncomfortable, but heavy, like the moment before a storm breaks. Then, gently, he asks, "Do you regret it? Helping them the other day?"

"No," I say, and it's the surest I've ever sounded. "Do you?"

He doesn't answer. Only reaches for another pomegranate from the tree, opening it as gently as he can so the juices don't spread all over his fingers. He handles these fruits—my fruits, technically—with such care that I can't help but admire him for it. Most would tear into the flesh and rip at the seeds, likes Hades did, but Thanatos takes the time and extra step to be gentle. Perhaps, because death can be so harsh, he tries to soften whatever he can.

We sit on the stone bench again, and eventually he says, "No. I don't regret it."

"Good. You shouldn't." We eat a few seeds in silence, then I ask, "When you reap the souls. Do many of them talk to you, like I did?"

Thanatos's voice softens. "Some beg. Some don't even realize it's over. But the ones who know, sometimes they thank me." He exhales. "Those are some of the hardest."

I glance sideways at him. "Why?"

He looks at me then, and I see it: that weight he carries so well most days, tucked behind his stern posture and his stillness. He wears it like armor, but tonight, it's looser on him.

"Because I'm not giving them peace," he says. "I'm just the threshold. They do the crossing on their own."

"You still guide them."

"No. They see what they want to see. You were a unique case. They see the last place they felt safe. Sometimes it's a face. Sometimes it's a smell, or a sound. One man heard his wife's humming. He followed it."

"That's beautiful," I say before I can stop myself.

Thanatos's eyes linger on me for a moment, then drop to his half of the pomegranate. "It was."

"I think they thank you because they're not alone. Because someone was there when everything else disappeared. Mortals, we're afraid of being alone. Of dying alone, especially."

His eyes find mine again. That look—still and unblinking— says things his mouth never would. Things I can't begin to name. I don't look away.

I don't *want* to look away.

It's warm in the garden, but not from the air. Not from the mist or the glowing blossoms. Just the proximity. He shifts, only slightly, and I feel the brush of his robe near my hand. Not quite a touch, but close enough to imagine it. I pull my knees up to my chest, suddenly aware of every inch of space between us. And how little of it I'd need to cross to feel his hand on mine.

"You don't just carry souls. You remember them."

He's still. Very still.

"You saw that man's wife, didn't you?"

He says nothing, but I see it in the way his fingers twitch.

"You carry pieces of them, even if you don't want to," I continue. "Even if you think you don't." He nods once, and just like that, it's too quiet again. After a few, long beats, I ask, "Have you ever told anyone this?"

"No. I'd never dare."

"Oh, Than." He moves through pain like it's a hallway he's memorized. But he feels it, I know he does—and for all his coldness, he's letting me see a piece of it tonight. I don't know what to do with that kind of trust, but I'm grateful for it.

"It's a job. Someone has to do it."

"That doesn't mean you have to be miserable. We can make it better. We can make this whole palace better."

"You think so?"

"I do. Give me time to think, and we can make it happen. I know it."

To my relief, when he looks at me, I see hope and belief in his eyes.

CHAPTER 8
THANATOS

As my brother rambles on, every word goes right in one ear and out the other. My mind is anywhere but his cave along the River Lethe, where we sit for our usual tea. Hypnos and I used to hate one another, but our mother encouraged us to have this family bonding every once in a while. As she is about most things, Nyx was right.

"You know, Than, I have never seen you so distracted." Hypnos takes a sip of his tea, pausing for the first time in gods only know how long. I don't know how the God of Sleep can be filled with so much energy all the time, talking as much as he does. Maybe it's because he sleeps enough for the both of us.

"My apologies. All the changes around here are disrupting my routine."

"Ah, with Her Majesty back?"

On instinct, my eyes narrow. "She doesn't want to be called that."

He holds his hands up defensively. "Whoa! Someone was quick to draw their sword there."

I sigh. "Yes, with Seph here, I'm distracted. What about it?"

"Well, it's not like you. You never were like the rest of us, you know. Taking partners and all that. And before you teleport away, which I know you're tempted to do," he's not wrong as he holds up a finger, "hear me out. Pretty please?"

"Fine."

"What's got you all perturbed?"

"If I tell you, you need to swear to me that this conversation doesn't leave this cave. Swear on Mother."

"Serious, huh?"

"Yes."

"I know that tone! Okay. I swear not only on Mother Nyx, but on Grandfather Chaos that I won't tell a single soul, god, or otherwise whatever it is you're about to say."

"Thank you." The only reason I even tell him is because we're in his private cave, separate from The Palace of Hades. Here, along the riverbanks, there are no prying eyes or ears. "She was reaped early."

"How early?"

"About seventy years."

My brother's eyes, the same opal shade as my own, bulge from above the rim of his teacup. "Damn, almost a whole human life."

"Something about this whole thing isn't sitting right with me. Now, you know I used to take issue with how some of the judgments were issued. I let that go ages ago. But Seph is taking issue, too. And the thing is, she's right. I can't tell her she's wrong. And when I look at her, it's like she's proof that the whole system might be fucked. Why would she be reaped early if not for Hades's selfishness?"

Hypnos runs a hand through his black curls, the same color as mine but much shorter. He inherited Nyx's features the same way I did, though his skin is a few shades darker than mine, comparable to slate. "Did you look at her file?"

"I did. And here's the thing: she lived a normal life. The one dark spot on her record's been pardoned. She's here now because he wants her to be. Given no one ever found out who killed Persephone, I can't shake this feeling that we're missing something."

"Do you think Hades maybe just wanted his wife back?"

"If he were so desperate for love, you'd think he'd find another mortal."

"He was never like Zeus and the others, and you know it. Maybe because you've never been in love, it's harder for you to understand."

My glare is instant. I see my own reflection in my tea, and I almost frighten even myself. "Don't give me that spiel, Hypnos."

"You're right, that wasn't fair of me. I'm sorry. I agree, though. Something's fishy. But what I'm curious about," he leans forward, propping his elbows on the table, "is why you're concerning yourself with these matters?"

"I've been asking myself the same damn question."

"You always got along with the Goddess of Spring, did you not?"

"I did. But we didn't see each other much."

"Because you were so busy with work? Or because you kept your distance?"

My jaw cracks as it sets. "Hypnos."

"Oh, come on. I'm sleepy, not stupid. I saw the way you used to look at Her Majesty. You know, some of the mortals whose dreams I tend to? They only have wet dreams about folks they're very close to. For others, they'll have them about strangers, famous people, you name it. Maybe you're more like the former. You need that connection first. So it's easier for you to sever it before it begins, hm?"

Even though he's right, I won't give him the satisfaction of saying so. "She's in a rough situation. I feel bad for her is all."

"Plenty of mortals wound up here as the result of a rough situation. So you go ahead and keep telling yourself that you don't have a crush on the Master's wife." He smirks. "It's only natural, after all. If you're Death, she's Life. Two sides of the same obol."

I respond too quickly. "She's not his wife. At least not anymore. Have you met her yet?"

"No, but I'd certainly like to. I've seen her in passing. She keeps to herself when she isn't training with the Furies or with you in her garden."

I did not expect to hear those words come out of his mouth in that order. "She's training with the Furies?"

"Oh, yeah! Gotten real chummy with them. I heard Alecto mention she they taught each other how to throw knives and use scythes. Good for her, I say!"

Good. Seph should be able to defend herself, especially here.

"You should introduce us," Hypnos continues. "It'll be good for her to have more friends. Especially if Hades is trying to win her back."

When I tell my brother about her past, about Nemesis's pardon, he whistles.

"Interesting! Even though she lost her memory, seems like she never lost the parts of her that hardened while she was here."

"No. But I think that's a good thing. We need real change around here. I'll introduce you. To your point, just because she can take care of herself doesn't mean she won't need friends."

"That's the spirit! Wow, Than. It's really good to see you coming around." He takes a moment to stir his tea, and the air shifts. "You know," he says, voice soft as drifting snow, "we're not built for this."

I arch a brow. "For what?"

68

He doesn't meet my eyes. Just keeps stirring. "For this. For needing, I guess."

The last bits of steam curl between us, turning the space hazy and intimate. The Palace feels a thousand miles away from this pocket of quiet, and I've never been more grateful for the distance he keeps here. This little pocket of safety.

"And yet, here we are."

Hypnos gives a sleepy, lopsided grin. "Here we are. Most men," his words are slow but deliberate, "either crack or calcify. There's no middle. No softness. No room."

My jaw tightens. I watch the tea leaf shavings at the bottom of my cup, as if it might answer.

"When we're little," he says, still not looking up, "they pat us on the head if we don't cry, if we don't cling. They call us strong. Then they forget us."

The words land heavy. True. Uncomfortable.

"I don't think they know what it costs," I say.

Hypnos's eyes lift, sharp despite his lazy slouch. "They don't care what it costs."

The light from the candles catches the flecks in his eyes. He looks so young like this, unguarded, like the brother I remember chasing shadows in the corners of the palace before we were old enough to receive our duties. Before Hades even ruled, when it was just Nyx and Erebus forming it within the Chaos.

"Do you ever feel..." I hesitate, the word thick on my tongue. "Lonely?"

He lets out a breath that's almost a laugh, but too hollow. "All the time. But it's worse because we're not supposed to name it. Worse because we can sit across from each other right now and still feel like we're bleeding alone."

The tea has gone lukewarm. I drink it anyway. Bitterness slides down my throat, heavy with honey and the remnants of the pomegranate flavor.

"It's not weakness," I say at last, voice low, a rasp I don't mean to share.

Hypnos blinks. "What isn't?"

"Wanting connection."

He holds my gaze for the first time, and in his eyes I see the same cavern I feel in my own chest—the endless echo of a truth we never speak aloud.

"No," he agrees. "It's not weakness."

We drink in silence for a moment. With the flick of his wrist, our team is warm again. His cave is still around us, the kind of quiet that could swallow a person whole. But we are not people, we are gods. We can handle it.

"I don't think the world knows what to do with men who want gentleness," Hypnos says finally, voice soft as sleep. "They flinch. Or mock. Or break us before we remember softness is even possible."

I study him, the easy slump of his shoulders, the bright flicker of thought in his eyes, the restless way his fingers drum against his cup. "We won't break," I say.

His mouth quirks faintly. "You're right."

Another silence blooms—not awkward, but rich, full of unsaid things. My brother and I can communicate like this, between the silences. We both know what it means to grow up in shadows, to carry blades in our hearts instead of hands, to know that fear can look like stone and grief can smell like tea.

"We should do this more often," I say. "Tea, that is."

"Well, for starters, you're actually drinking this time." His lips curl in a tease, his usual light nature back. "But I'm glad to hear you say that. That palace, I can't stand it. Too stuffy. Makes me sleep with one eye open. You're welcome here any time." Hypnos tips his cup toward me in a slow, almost solemn toast. "To staying soft despite it all."

I tip mine back. The candlelight catches the dark red surface of the tea.

"To staying soft despite it all," I echo.

Our cups touch with a quiet clink that sounds almost like a promise. And for a single, shivering breath, the loneliness from the last few centuries feels less like a curse and more like something we can survive together.

CHAPTER 9
THANATOS

Persephone walks at my side a few days later, close enough that her shoulder brushes my arm every few steps. I wonder if she knows I notice. I wonder if she knows I count them—the moments she leans close, each time her fingers twitch as if debating whether to reach for mine, every quiet exhale when she lets herself trust the silence between us.

"They'll be kind," I murmur.

She gives me a quick glance. "You don't know that."

"I do. It's been a long time since I've visited, but I know my family well enough."

She studies me for a heartbeat longer, then exhales. "I believe you."

We enter the transportation circle together, the bridge from here to Chaos. Hades built it for my mother a long time ago, so she could tend to all her realms with ease and efficiency.

Starlight spills out across the threshold. It's not cold or sharp, but soft and silver-blue, like moonlight caught in still water. The chamber is vast but never empty. Every time I return, it feels like stepping into memory. Into a place I can call home with love, not disdain like the palace.

Nyx is already here, seated gracefully on a curved chaise of spun night. No sign of my father, but Hypnos lounges on a cloudlike bench that keeps drifting gently to the left, which he hasn't noticed.

There is no denying my mother's presence. As the night, any light is swallowed the moment she enters a room. It's comforting, though. I don't fear the dark, never have, and I don't think Seph will, either. When I look at Seph, she's still glowing like spring, and doesn't curl in on herself. Her whole body is relaxed. She's safe, and she knows it.

"My sweet girl." Nyx's voice is everything it always is: calm, deep, beautiful. This time, there's warmth beneath it. "I am so sorry we did not get to formally meet until now. I wish I had more time the day of your arrival."

My mother embraces Seph, who accepts the hug in an instant. My mother does not move, and sends me a glance of empathy. Seph needs this maternal embrace, more than she's let on. My mother will allow Seph to be the one to end the hug, not breaking until Seph is ready.

"It is an honor to meet you, unfortunate as the circumstances may be."

"Thank you, ma'am."

"Please. Nyx is fine. My son has told me such wonderful things about you, including that you wish to drop all formalities. If I am not to call you by any titles, then the same shall be true for me."

"I can see where Thanatos gets his manner of speech from."

Even I chuckle. "Yes, Mother Nyx has had quite the influence on me."

My mother continues, "I'm glad you've come."

"You are?"

"Very. Thanatos doesn't often bring anyone to us. He doesn't let people in. You must be significant to him."

I shoot her a glance, warning her to watch it. I don't want to scare Seph off.

My father enters the room just as Seph breaks away from Nyx. Erebus bears the same lichen complexion as I do, and is where Hypnos and I get our dark hair. Whereas our mother's is all curls, which we've inherited from her, Erebus's is a straight braid running down his back. We have Nyx's face, but Erebus's eyes.

Erebus inclines his head. "So this is the girl the whole damn Underworld is talking about."

"A pleasure to meet you. Erebus, I presume?"

"She knows us."

"Did before I reaped her," I say. "Knew me right off the bat, too."

Hypnos yawns. "Don't most?"

"By my real name. I'm barely called that by anyone from outside of Greece on the surface these days, and it's been like that for centuries."

"It's no wonder you like her so much, son. So, girl, you think you're equipped to kiss Death? Think you can handle it?"

Seph stiffens. I open my mouth. But before any of us can speak, Nyx lifts a hand. "Erebus."

He says nothing else, only settles back into his usual lounge chair.

Seph finds her poise again fast, like a blade being sheathed. "I do. Though I'm not sure whether you mean that literally or metaphorically."

Hypnos and Erebus both snort.

"She's funny," my father says. "You didn't say she was funny."

Seph gives me a look that silently tells me she doesn't get the joke.

"I didn't think I had to," I reply.

"She's also very pretty," Hypnos whispers—loudly—behind his hand.

"Hypnos," Nyx barks.

He shrinks into his seat. "I was complimenting!"

Seph's cheeks flush. I don't look directly at her. I don't need to; the warmth in her presence is already tingling against my arm.

"I brought her here because she matters. To me." It's harder than I expect to say aloud. Not because it isn't true, but because it is. Because no one has mattered to me like she does.

Nyx watches me for a long, slow moment. Then she turns her gaze to Seph.

"You have returned to a palace that was not built for you," she says. "You carry names that no longer fit. And yet, you remain."

"You could say that."

Nyx nods once at her. "Then I hope you will continue. What do you plan to do, now that you're here?"

"It's okay," I say. "There are no ears or eyes here, out in the abyss of Chaos. Whatever we say stays here."

Seph nods and grabs my hand, squeezing it tight. "I want to take down Hades. I don't have the specifics yet. But I'm working on it. I've killed before. I can do it again."

This catches my father's attention. "Well, why didn't you lead with that?"

"It wasn't something I did for fun. A friend of mine... someone hurt her. They hurt her in all of the worst ways you can hurt a woman, and she was the one who had to pay for it. Not him. She suffered, still suffers on the surface, and he walked. I couldn't let him hurt anyone else. So no, I don't regret taking the scythe I used to harvest my family's lavender fields and turning it into a weapon. Nor do I regret staging the accident that let me get away with it."

As Seph tells the story, she holds her head high. The conviction in her eyes is strong as she continues, "I'm a goddess turned mortal turned goddess again who got away with murder once. I can get away with it again. I may carry a sunny disposition, but all the better to let Hades underestimate me with. Don't get me wrong, I know I can't do this overnight. But I can do it if you give me time."

Nyx asks, "And who would rule the Underworld in his stead?"

"I would. Persephone was the queen, right? And I'm her. I've ruled it once. I can do it again."

Erebus grins. "I like her a lot."

Hypnos excuses himself, rambling something about making us all tea. Mother uses the opportunity to usher us into her sitting room. It's a patchwork of shadows and starlight, like someone tried to carve a drawing room out of the edge of the night sky. Comfortable chairs float just above the floor. Hypnos presents our tea service on a table that's probably older than the mortal realm, then naps in the corner. Seph takes it all in with wide, careful eyes.

Across from us, Erebus leans back in his obsidian armchair like it's a throne. He has one leg kicked up over the armrest. "I remember the first Titan I felled," he says, apropos of nothing. "Massive brute. Four heads. Breath smelled like molten ash and desperation. I crushed his ribcage with my bare hands."

Seph raises an eyebrow.

"Oh," Erebus adds quickly, "metaphorically bare. I wore armor. Mostly shadows. Very intimidating."

Nyx sighs delicately. "Darling, that was not a Titan. That was your reflection in a dark pool after too much nectar."

Erebus throws up a hand. "Details."

Seph hides her smile behind the rim of her teacup. I can feel it, and wish I could capture it.

"Father," I say carefully, "we invited Seph to get to know us. Not to be inducted into your mythology."

"Pah!" he scoffs. "What is family if not the sharing of heroic feats? She should know what lineage she's flirting with."

Seph nearly chokes on her tea.

"Flirting?" I echo, my voice as flat as I can manage.

Nyx does not intervene.

Erebus leans forward with a dramatic gleam in his eye. "My son here, this one," he gestures to me, "tall, brooding, blades for days with that scythe. He barely even spoke for the first few centuries of his existence. No one could get a word out of him. But then she arrives," he gestures grandly at Seph, "in the Underworld after Hades takes her and suddenly, he's talking. Laughing, even."

Seph looks at me, eyes wide and dazzling as she asks, "Really?" It makes something in my chest loosen.

"Yes, really!" Erebus drains his goblet and slams it down, though it makes no sound, only a ghostly thump. "She's good for you, son."

"I don't know what you're talking about."

Seph glances between us, her voice gentle when she speaks. "You're still helping me find my place here. But I'm glad to know *yours* isn't all scythes and scowling."

I huff a breath. "It's mostly scowling."

Erebus claps his hands. "A family resemblance, then!" Nyx gives him a look that could dim the stars, and he shrugs. "What? I'm charming. You married me."

"I *created* you."

My father shrugs. "A minor detail."

Seph leans slightly toward me. In a whisper, she asks, "Is this how it always is?"

"This is better than usual."

"I like it," she whispers back.

I glance down at her hand resting near mine on the armrest. I don't touch it, not here, not now. But she catches the flicker of the movement, and her fingers nudge closer. Barely. A breath of space between us. Whatever we're dancing toward is dangerous, but it sends my heart fluttering all the same.

Erebus raises his teacup again. "To new beginnings! And strange girls from above who somehow tolerate my son."

Seph grins. "I think I scare him more than he scares me, sometimes."

"You should." Nyx sips her tea with regal composure. "He's never been good with the living."

"I'm not exactly living anymore."

"You're still more alive than the rest of the damned palace," Nyx says. There's something in her tone: not pity, not warning, but quiet recognition. A kind of knowing Seph meets with equal calm.

"I'll try not to break anything," Seph says.

Erebus waves a hand. "Break what you like. Rules are just decorations. Unless you break *me*, of course, which would be tragic."

Nyx leans in. "That wouldn't take much these days."

He gasps. "My love."

Seph turns to me, that smile still in her voice. "They're incredible."

"They're exhausting."

"You're all... very real. Like a real family."

I glance sideways at her, and even in front of all of them, I let the corner of my mouth curl. "So are you."

Nyx then says, "I'd love to chat with Seph alone, if that's alright. Seph is what you like to be called, yes?" When she nods, Nyx stands, offering a hand to Seph. "Come with me."

Seph gives my arm a reassuring pat, letting me know she'll be okay. My mother leads her, arm-in-arm, to the back patio. Once they're gone, my father stands up, then ushers me along.

"Come. I know a good spot for eavesdropping."

We shouldn't, but I don't protest. I can't deny I'm not curious.

Outside, Nyx and Seph pass beneath an arch woven of black-violet flowers. From our spot against the wall near the window, my father has identified a slit in the wood where we can hear into the outside of the Chaos realm.

"I didn't expect all of you to be so..." Seph trails off.

"Loud?" Nyx offers.

"Normal. Warm. Not literally, but you know what I mean."

Nyx hums low, a sound like stars rearranging. "Death is often mistaken for coldness. It is not. It is stillness. Stillness can be full of love."

"I was afraid to meet you," Seph admits.

"And now?"

"Now I'm afraid you'll see right through me."

Nyx stops beside a softly glowing basin. Within it, stars flicker and fade in slow spirals. I've walked by the basin countless times. She turns to Seph. "I see into you, sweet girl. Not through. What's on your mind?"

"I don't want to be Persephone. Not because I hate her or anything. But I don't know if she ever chose this life. Or this realm. Or that crown."

"You fear she was made, not born."

"Something like that."

Nyx dips her fingers into the starlit basin. "My dear," she

says softly, "when you came to the Underworld the first time, you were a bright light wrapped in certainty. You knew yourself. Asked so many questions, and walked through walls meant to keep you out."

"That doesn't sound like me now."

"Doesn't it, though? Thanatos has told me how you question our system. And you yourself told us you are working out a plan to stop Hades himself." She lifts her hand from the basin. One star lingers on her fingertip, then fades. "You do not have to be what others expect," she continues. "Even the gods are allowed to change. Have confidence in yourself, real confidence. Don't let it waver."

"I want to. But it feels like standing at the edge of something too wide to name."

"Good," Nyx replies. "That's where everything important begins."

"Thanatos," Seph then says, and Nyx turns, listening. "We're dancing toward something, but I don't know what. He's been a wonderful friend to me. Is it strange, though, for me to wish for more? Hades pursues me, yet when I dream, it's not of him. It's of your son."

"He is afraid of hope. It's a rare thing in him. Fragile. But he has never turned from you."

"No. He always finds me."

She smiles, not wide, but a secret pressed between her and the dark. "Give him time, then. He'll come around. You belong, Seph. Not because of your name. Not because of who you were. But because you're here."

The revelation stuns me, even though I suspected it. Hearing it verbally confirmed shakes me, and my head begins to swirl. Before I can think about it too much, my father claps me on the shoulder.

"We should go back. Best not test our luck."

Father and I return to the lounge, sipping another cup of tea. Hypnos has drifted off to his room already, leaving us alone.

Erebus asks, "Since when do you actually drink tea, by the way?"

"You can thank her. She got me to start eating."

"Oh, you love her, don't you?" When I don't answer, my father laughs, a booming sound that rattles his teacup. "My son, I am no fool. Loving someone another seeks to claim is no easy feat. Be careful, yeah?"

"I'm always careful."

"I know you are. Still worth saying."

We drink our second cup in silence until Seph and Nyx return. Nyx bids us goodnight, bringing my father with her to their bedroom, leaving me alone with Seph.

"Can we stay here tonight?" Her eyes are wide, pleading. "I don't want to return to the palace. Not yet. So rarely do I feel safe enough to actually sleep, and..."

"We can. If Hades asks, Nyx will cover for you."

"Thank you. This means so much to me."

"We don't have an extra guest room. Mother and Father left my bedroom for me, though I don't think I've used it in centuries. They'll be thrilled for someone to stay there." I remember what she said to Nyx, then ask, "Would you like me to stay with you, or would you like to be alone?"

Seph doesn't hesitate. "Of course I want you here. We don't have to do anything, and no one has to know. Just... Please. Don't leave me alone."

Unable to help myself, I brush a strand of her curls behind her ear. "Your wish is my command." I want so badly to pull her close to me, to kiss her, to scream that Hades can't have her because I love her and she's mine to protect.

But instead, I lead her to my undecorated chambers, where we curl up in peaceful silence next to one another. I don't sleep, but Seph does the moment her head lands against my chest. A tenderness overwhelms me, and I wish I could freeze this moment. What I'd give for us to stay here, safely cocooned in Chaos and one another. I stroke her hair as she sleeps, until, for the first time in forever, I doze off.

Maybe rest isn't so bad after all.

CHAPTER 10
SEPH

I return from the Chaos realm feeling rejuvenated. Having friends is a relief, especially ones I can trust. To feel the love of a mother again, to hear the laughter of a family, made me feel more at home than I have in ages. I'm not sure how much time has passed since I died—it moves so strangely here, it's impossible to tell.

But what I told Thanatos's family, that I want to stop Hades, is a conviction that burns in my chest. It leads me to the archives a few days later, guarded by Megaera today. She lets me in without question, only a smile and a pat on my shoulder. Her presence is reassuring, even though I'm still not completely certain I can trust her yet like I can Thanatos and his family.

As I peruse the shelves, unraveling scrolls and sifting through tomes, I can hear Megaera speaking from the other side of the door.

I freeze. The book in my hands incriminates me, and I need to put it away immediately. I don't have time to make a mistake, but I need to finish this tome, meaning a repeat trip is necessary.

The Titanomachy rests between my palms, the thick text

heavy with ancient rituals once used to bind gods. I've read in great detail how the gods killed the Titans, looking for ideas to get rid of my Hades problem. Some of the scrolls detailed similar, but not quite what I needed. This will require something more clever, more intricate than a scythe. All I've learned is more about adamant, the material from the dagger that killed the past version of me.

"Yes, Persephone is in there. But Her Majesty requested to not be disturbed."

Hades' deep rumble of a voice raises enough for me to hear him now. "And why, pray tell, would that be?"

"She's hoping to jog her memory." I'm grateful to Megaera for lying for me. "That requires the utmost concentration."

"As the ruler of this palace and as your master, I demand you let me through at once."

"Before I do, Lord Hades, may I say something?"

He groans. "Watch your tongue, Megaera. But yes."

I take the opportunity to put the book back and swap it for a random book. I take a quick glance at the cover: *Songs by Orpheus and Eurydice*. Perfect. Even if Megaera can't get Hades to go away, she's done me a great favor in buying me time.

"If you wish to earn her favor and trust, then let her be. She needs the space to adapt. Once she's more comfortable, she'll come to you, I'm sure."

"I cannot risk that she doesn't. Now step aside or suffer the consequences. Don't you have souls to torture?"

She scoffs. "Fine. But don't say I didn't warn you."

The room was already hot, but it practically starts steaming as soon as the door opens and Hades enters. Even with him behind me, his shadow dominates the room, impossible to ignore or miss. The few shades working here all freeze, stopping to bow or bend a knee. I do no such thing, despite the way I feel my throat closing in fear.

I straighten instinctively, spine taut. He's there at the end of the row, shadows pooling around his boots like they know he belongs to them. He moves closer, each step slow, deliberate. His gaze pins me in place. His red eyes are as dark as a fresh grave, mouth curved in something that wants to be a smile but curdles halfway.

"Persephone," he says, like he's tasted the word and found it saccharine. "I've been looking for you."

My mouth goes dry. "My Lord."

He watches me, head tilting slightly. "You've been busy."

I nod, small, careful. "There's so much to learn."

He tuts softly, a sound that slides under my skin. "You don't need old stories. Anything you wish to know, you need only ask me."

He takes another step, and another, until the world narrows to the shelves at my back and him at my front. His presence presses the air from my lungs.

"I wouldn't want to waste your time," I say, words breathless, small. "You have the whole Underworld to rule, after all."

He leans forward, shadows dancing across his face. His eyes flick down, lingering on my lips before returning to mine. "And yet here I am," he says, almost gently. "Making time for you."

Hades moves closer, too close. The scent of smoke and old stone clings to him. My instincts are screaming at me, and I fight not to run. My heart is hammering so hard it hurts.

"I'm grateful."

"Are you?" His voice is softer than silk, but it cuts deeper than any blade. "Because I see you. I watch you wandering these halls with your quiet questions. Your eyes full of doubts. I wonder... are you grateful for what I offer? Or do you wish to escape me?"

I swallow hard. My hands shake where I clutch the book of songs. "I don't wish to escape." Not that I have a choice.

He lifts a hand, brushing a stray lock of hair from my cheek. His fingers are hot and perfectly steady. The touch is feather-light, but it might as well be a shackle, and I flinch before I can stop myself. "You flinch from me," he murmurs. "I can feel your fear. You don't have to hide here, you know," he murmurs, voice as smooth and dark as polished onyx. "This palace is yours, too."

I try to smile. It feels brittle. "I'm not hiding. Just studying."

He hums low, like he doesn't believe me, like he's the only one allowed to define my motives. His eyes sweep over the table, the unfurled scrolls of diagrams of seals and binding circles that I forgot about. *Shit.* His mouth tightens.

"Such dangerous reading," he murmurs, voice like a blade sheathed in velvet. "Are you planning something unwise?"

I force a laugh, light and bright and false. "Of course not. I don't even know what those symbols are, and I'm still learning Greek."

I can read Greek fluently, but Hades doesn't need to know that.

Hades steps closer still. I back up until I feel the shelves behind me. He looms, blocking the lantern light, shadows wrapping around him like a lover. His smile is gone now. In its place is hunger—both for my body and my compliance. Men like him aren't used to be told no. Consequences are dire for such a thing.

"Do you know what I see when I look at you?" he whispers, voice so soft I have to strain to catch it.

I swallow hard. "What do you see?"

He raises a hand again, this time brushing a lock of hair behind my ear. I hate that I shiver. I hate that my skin feels tight, like it might crack under his touch.

"I see what was mine," he says, voice low and reverent. "What should be mine again."

My phantom heart pounds so loudly I think he can hear it. "You already know I don't remember being anyone's."

His eyes flicker, something cruel passing through them like a storm cloud. "Memory is irrelevant. How many times must I say it? You are here."

I search desperately for an out—a polite excuse, a place to run—but the aisle feels miles long, and he's already filled it with his presence.

"I'm grateful for your welcome," I say softly, voice trembling just enough to sound sincere, "but I need more time to adjust."

His gaze softens by degrees, but it's a predator's softness. A lion before the pounce. "Adjust," he repeats, tasting the word. "I understand."

He doesn't move. Neither do I. We stand locked in silence, the space between us thick as old blood. I feel my breathing quicken, the air tearing in and out of my lungs like I'm drowning.

"I'll give you time," he says at last, but there's an edge to it. A promise or a threat, I can't tell. "But don't mistake patience for indifference. I'll be watching."

He steps back, just enough that I can slip around him. I seize the chance like its life itself, skirting past without looking up. I feel the heat of his gaze on my back, the weight of his attention following me even as I flee down the row. Along the way, I drop the book on a random table, wanting to be rid of it.

I don't stop until I'm out of the archives. Hades wants me, and there is nothing in the world that terrifies me more.

CHAPTER 11
SEPH

I don't remember crossing the palace. I don't remember
the halls, the gargoyle statues, the tall columns.

All I remember is the cold in my veins, the way
Hades's eyes felt like iron bands locking around my throat. The
way his words still echo: *I'll be watching.*

I don't want to be watched.

I want to be found.

I run to the garden, my only sanctuary in the palace. The
vines don't care who I used to be. The roots don't remember my
past. Even the blossoms open for me without asking for
anything in return. That's more than I can say for most of the
palace. I walk the stone path in bare feet, letting the cold bite
just enough to remind me I'm still real.

I all but stumble past the gates, shadows slipping over me
like cool water in the desert. My heart feels too big for my ribs,
thundering wildly, refusing to quiet even after death. I didn't
think the old thing could even beat anymore, but Hades is that
frightening.

Thanatos is already here, sitting beneath the pale branches

of a pomegranate tree, one knee drawn up, arms resting loose, as if he's part of the garden itself.

He says my name, voice low, rougher than I've ever heard it.

I can't speak as I cross the stones in a handful of shaky steps, hands trembling, breath ragged. His stands, arms opening without thought, catching me against his chest. The grass is warm beneath my fingers, but the chill radiates off him as the cold silk of his cloak surrounds me. A welcome relief. Steady, solid, real.

"Did he—" he starts, but I shake my head wildly against him, fists twisting in his robe.

"I just needed you," I whisper. The words break like glass. "Please."

His arms tighten. Thanatos lowers his head until his forehead brushes mine, breath mingling. I can smell the faint sweetness of pomegranate on him, the faint chill of the night clinging to his skin.

"I'm here," he says. Two simple words, but they mean the world to me.

I tilt my head up, eyes finding his. I catch the colorful flecks in his irises as his gaze drops to my mouth, then snaps back up —his breath hitching like he's fighting himself.

I realize I owe him an explanation. "I went into the archives today." He waits, so I continue, "I found records. Old ones. About the war. About how they stopped the Titans. How they sealed them."

"You shouldn't be reading those." From his flat tone, I can tell he doesn't mean it.

"Too late," I say. "Were you waiting for me?"

He hums low in his throat. "I don't sleep, so I've taken to coming here."

"Wait. You don't sleep ever?"

"No. Except for when we stayed in Chaos. That was the first time in a long time."

"Did you dream?" I ask.

"No. Also never."

I need so badly to talk about my own that I press anyway. "What about daydreams?"

"That implies I have time to imagine things that aren't real."

"I think dreams are real," I counter. "Or at least the wanting in them is." He's quiet again, so I go on. "I haven't told anyone else this. But I'm getting my memories back. Mel is visiting me at night."

"Melinoë?"

"Yes. They're not my memories exactly, since mine are all lost. Can't exactly pluck them out of the Lethe. But we're working with what we can. To break it up, since they're awful, your brother's been helping me. Every other night, I dream of home. Of the lavender fields overlooking the mountains." I pause before I confess, "Sometimes, I dream of you there with me. In those fields. I did that night in Chaos, too."

Thanatos's expression isn't quite skeptical, but there's caution there.

I dare to ask, "Do you feel this connection between us, or is it one-sided on my end?"

"My brother suspects its due to our powers. Life and death. I've felt it since I met you." His eyes shift, and I can sense him getting ready to flee again, but I fist his clothes tighter.

"Please stay. Why do you always leave so suddenly?"

His body tightens, even though he doesn't pull away. "Because if I stay too long, I start wanting things."

I swallow, feeling the tension build in my chest. In the pit of my stomach, too. "What kind of things?"

He shudders. His thumb brushes the corner of my mouth,

hesitant, reverent, as if he's waiting for the world to end. He drops his gaze and doesn't look at me. I don't think he can as he says, "Things I'm not meant to want."

"According to who?"

"You already know."

Of course I do, but it doesn't stop me. "Do you want to know what I dream of us doing in those lavender fields?"

Because I suspect what he wants is the same thing I do.

"Tell me."

"I dream of us lying in the fields together. The sun shines on us. Your lips explore my bare skin. So do your hands."

When he whispers my name, it's like he's pleading. It's a tone of his voice I've never heard before, and I want to hear it again, and again, and forever.

"Should I stop?"

"You should. But I don't want you to." Those opal eyes shimmer with longing. If I'd known Death looked like this, I would have been far less afraid of him in life. "And that scares the shit out of me."

"What if I don't want to stop, either?"

"We both know why we shouldn't do this. Why this would be forbidden."

That one word—*forbidden*—is enough to build upon the tension I feel deep in my core. I've never yearned for someone before, not truly, not until now. Not until I had that first dream of us in the lavender fields. In this dark, dreary place, Thanatos provides a safe place to rest. I feel a deep-seated desire to do so in his arms, much like I did in Chaos.

"Besides," Thanatos continues, "I wouldn't even begin to know what to do."

"Do we need to know what we're doing? Can't we simply be, and figure it out along the way? I'm no one's wife. No one's bride. Only a lavender farmer."

Thanatos cups my face with his hand and stares at my lips. His touch is so gentle it nearly makes me weep. Perhaps it's because I have known death, have slayed a man with my own scythe-wielding hands, that I can trust Thanatos so wholly. That I do not fear him like I do the others. He is a familiar comfort, one I've worked alongside in secret. It is no different now than it was then, not truly.

"I have never known want," he whispers, "until I met you."

My heart soars at the confession. "You don't need to want me. I'm yours for the taking."

"Not everyone would agree with you."

"Does that even matter?"

"Yes. Power here is a delicate hierarchy."

"A hierarchy that you sit atop."

"One *he* sits atop."

"And you right alongside him. He can't run this place without you and your work. You've said so yourself. Don't forget that. You have power here, too."

We're a mere breath away from one another. I want nothing more than to close the gap, but I heed Nyx's advice since I don't want to scare Thanatos away.

Thanatos whispers, "Tell me to stop. Tell me I'm crossing a line and that my being this close scares you."

"I can't. That would be a lie, and I don't want to lie to you."

"Tell me I repulse you. That I strike fear in your heart."

"Quite the contrary."

"Tell me not to kiss you."

"Than, I want you to kiss me. I want that more than anything."

Shadows swirl around us, obscuring any who might see should they walk by the garden. They aren't pressing or thick enough to obstruct my vision, but they'll do the trick to protect us from prying eyes. Only then, Thanatos finally closes the gap, pressing our lips together.

His kiss is a contradiction: cold enough to make me shiver, but sending a warmth through me all the same. Cautious and gentle with an underlying passion and desire for more. Thanatos's fingers graze my face like I'm some fragile pottery, the same way he handles the pomegranates, yet his lips move on mine like he wants to consume me—and by the gods, I *want* him to consume me. We toe a line and dive into the deep end all the same.

After a few seconds of this, of being lost in one another, he tugs me closer to him by my waist. I find his hair, tangling my fingers in the depths of black waves, and he honest to gods moans in my mouth. I do not know if love can exist in a place like this, but Death has welcomed me with open arms, showed me gentleness and beauty in the dark, and I crave him like a drug before our lips even part.

But after a moment—a long moment, but too short, as contradictory as his kiss—Thanatos pulls away. His eyes are wide, with terror and realization and shock all at once. I can see it in the way the rainbow specks flicker in the darkness, all the brighter due to the contrast.

Before I can say anything, Thanatos disappears along with his cloud of shadow, leaving me standing alone in The Garden of Pomegranates. The sudden absence of him, after finally giving in to such a small fraction of our desires, feels like my soul's been cleaved. Perhaps this is my punishment, my karma for taking a life no matter how wretched.

This is the Underworld. There's no happiness here.

CHAPTER 12
THANATOS

The work never ends. That should be a comfort. Spirits fall like rain in Asphodel. Lists stretch longer than eternity. Fields of punishment swell with names, all desperate for a verdict. I throw myself into the harvest, and for once, I hate every moment of it.

She's in every pause. Every silence. Every heartbeat between names.

Seph.

Her mouth, soft against mine. The warmth of her hands on my face. The way she didn't flinch when I leaned in, didn't pull away, didn't look confused or afraid. She wanted it.

And I—I wanted her.

Gods.

I've never wanted someone before. Not like this. Not physically, not desperately, not with this ache that sits low in my spine and tight in my throat. Desire was always something that belonged to mortals. Weakness wrapped in fire. I watched others fall to it and pitied them.

Now I can't even close my eyes without seeing the way she looked at me after. As if I was something more than death.

It terrifies me.

So I do the only thing I know how: I disappear.

I leave before she enters a room. I take assignments across the furthest reaches of the Underworld. I arrive on the surface and spend too long reaping. Hypnos jokes that I've become "weird and twitchy" when we have tea next. The Fury sisters avoid me entirely.

I keep my distance for seventeen days. I count them.

And every day, I still find her. Not up close, but from across the training yard, or down a corridor, or at the garden gates. I catch glimpses of her in the archives, curled over some dusty tome, eyes lit with purpose. I listen for her voice and find it woven into conversations with Megaera, with Alecto, even with my brother now.

But not me. Never me. Not since that night. I make sure of that.

Until finally, I have nothing left to hide behind. No distractions, no more missions.

So I go to the one person who sees through me always: Nyx.

Her chambers are quiet, dark as breath. Starlight spills between the curtains, scattered with slow-moving constellations. She is as she always is—regal, unreadable, woven from shadow.

She doesn't look up when I enter. "Thanatos."

"Mother."

There is no use pretending. She lifts her eyes, and they land on me like truth made flesh. "You are troubled."

I stand before her, arms crossed, posture rigid. "It's nothing."

Her smile is the kind that knows better. "You wouldn't have come to me in Chaos if it was nothing. You have been gone from yourself for weeks."

I clench my jaw.

She waits.

Finally, I breathe out. "I kissed her."

Nyx blinks, only once. "Ah."

"I didn't mean to."

"Of course you didn't." She's not sarcastic, and I don't know if I find that relieving or not.

"She... she didn't pull away. She looked at me like she saw me." My voice shakes. I hate that it shakes. "And now I can't stop thinking about it. About her." Nyx is quiet. I look away, suddenly furious at myself for even bringing this up. "It was a mistake."

"Was it?"

I grit my teeth. "I don't have the luxury of desire, Mother. I am *Death*. I am not meant for softness. I am not meant to want."

She rises from her chair like mist unfolding. "Thanatos," she says, stepping toward me. "My son. You were shaped by shadow, but your soul is not a void."

"I kissed her," I whisper. "And now I don't know what to do or what that makes me."

Nyx's voice is gentle. "You are what you have always been. But you are also more. Do not fear that."

"I'm not afraid of changing," I lie.

"You are," she says, without judgment. "And that is all right."

We stand in silence. I press my fingers into the curve of my palm, grounding myself.

"Hades..." I can't even finish the sentence, the thought, any of it.

"She is not married to him, not anymore. And she deserves someone who sees her," Nyx says softly. "And you already do."

I look at her.

She smiles. "Go to her. Let her choose."

The words root in my chest. *Let her choose.* That's all I ever want to give her: a choice. I nod once and vanish from the chamber in a cloud of darkness. But this time, for the first time in weeks, I don't run away from her.

I go to find her.

I check the Garden of Pomegranates first, sticking to the shadows. If she isn't here, I don't want to draw the attention of whoever may be. The only one here is Hades, sitting at a stone bench—*our* stone bench, I initially think, even though I've no right to the thought—with a pomegranate in his large hand. He's ripped it open, but with no delicacy or care. Even from where I stand, I can see the jagged edges of each half and how the juices stain his fingers, dripping down his hands and wrists in red streaks.

Though I am shrouded in shadows, Hades can move through the darkness as efficiently as I can. Not wanting to test my luck, I vanish before I'm spotted, checking my next location. I find Seph in her chambers.

She's sprawled atop her bed with her robe hiked up to her waist. Her legs are spread, and her fingers hover over the space between her legs. With her index finger bent to rub at the apex, her middle finger dips in and out of her folds. I can see them glisten on the extraction.

Something within me snaps.

I've seen people have sex before. The gods are known to partake in more sex than most mortals can fathom. While I am no stranger to the concept, I've yet to participate myself.

No interest. Too busy reaping souls to care to develop an interest, too.

But something about Seph, the way her hair sprawls out behind her in soft curls, the relaxed look on her face—a look I've only otherwise seen her have around me—has my cock stiffening beneath my short chiton.

Part of me is tempted to reach into my robe, to fist my cock and experiment with stroking it. Though I am hidden in the darkness, it feels wrong to do so as I watch, like some sick voyeur. Seph has been through a lot, is going through a lot, with Hades actively pursuing her. I do not wish to stoop to his level by touching myself for the first time while watching her without her knowing.

And yet, I am glued to the spot. Mesmerized by the sight of her self pleasure, I can't stop watching.

The unthinkable happens.

Seph calls my name. It's a faint whisper, a breathy moan, and I freeze. I'm still hidden in the shadows, so there's no way she sees me. While I normally run cold, my skin feels hotter than Tartarus when she calls my name for a second time.

It's impossible for her to see me, yet she pauses what she's doing. I hear the slickness of her when she withdraws her hand, and I don't understand why I desire to run my mouth over her wet finger. Seph only breaks to remove her robe entirely, revealing her body to me.

She is finer than any artwork. While her legs and arms still show muscle tone from years on the farm and training with the Furies, she's otherwise all soft curves and plush features that I yearn to sink my teeth into like no other.

Once Seph disposes of the garment, leaving herself bare on her black silk sheets, she resumes her ministrations. This time, her other hand cups her breast, rolling her nipple between two fingers. But above all else, it's the way she says my name that causes my cock to twitch. It's stiffer than ever as I hear the trust and desire in her voice. And as I think of the inner workings of this woman, this sweet soul who is capable of wielding a scythe to cultivate harvest or to reap a soul herself as I might, I can see that bond. How life and death are intertwined, so of course, we are too. It fills me with a yearning for her so intense it aches.

I still do not dare touch myself. No matter how heavy my balls feel, nor how much my cock throbs at the sight of her, I can't allow myself to cross this threshold yet. Just when I think I am in the clear, that she did not see me after all and her undressing was a mere coincidence, Seph whimpers my name for a third time.

And as she does, she stares right at me.

"Than, I know you're lurking there, somewhere. Please, come out from hiding. I promise I'm not mad."

It would be so easy to vanish, to teleport away and pretend I was never here, never saw anything. So, so easy.

Yet I don't.

Instead, I move forward, my footsteps silent. Seph, to my surprise, doesn't stop. Perhaps, if she knows I've been watching her, doesn't see a point in stopping.

"I'm sorry I've been avoiding you. I wasn't sure how to handle what last happened between us."

"All is forgiven. Would you care to join me? No need to hide. I removed the scrying tools he left in my chambers, so no one will know. Only us."

It's a tempting offer.

"You don't mind that I've been watching you?"

"No, but only because it's you."

Something about her words clicks it all in to place for me. I'm still hesitant, but I join her by kneeling on the end of her bed.

I tell her, "You're stunning." It doesn't feel like enough.

She blushes all the same, especially as I bring my hand beneath my chiton. I'm not sure I'm ready to bare myself completely, so I keep it on as I fist my cock.

"Show me how you like it." I mean to ask, but comes out more like a demand.

Seph doesn't seem to mind, a coy smile playing at her lips.

My eyes dart between her beautiful, blissed out face and her glistening cunt, pink and pretty as her fingers dip in and out.

Even as I mentally tell myself I shouldn't, I pump myself to the same lazy rhythm as her fingers and ask, "Did you know I was there the whole time?"

"I did. I sensed the shift the moment you arrived."

There is no point in asking her how. Whatever this bond we have is must be the reason, and I'm too drunk on her to question it. "Is that why you took your robe off? So I could have a better look?"

"Yes. Before you got here, I'd been thinking of you. I haven't stopped thinking about you, Than."

I groan as I increase the pressure around my head, careful not to pinch the silver ring there. I pierced myself there after I ran out of room on my ears, enjoying the aesthetic appeal— even if only I would see it. Now, Seph might, too. Not today. But if I continued to lose my self control like this, she'd know of it in the near future.

Not that I minded losing my self control when it was just us. No scrying, no potential prying eyes, but just us. Life and Death, together as they should be.

"No matter the pace," Seph says, "I love a lot of pressure on my clit. Do you like it on your head, too?"

Any attempt at speech results in a moan of some sort. I nod my assent. When she asks if I edged myself, I nod again. Even though it wasn't intentional, it is the truth. It's all so new to me, my head is spinning. I'm not entirely positive this isn't a strange dream my brother's put me under in order to stop running and confront my feelings. But when I blink, she's still there, still playing with herself and staring right at me like she wants me.

And I can't ignore how much I want her. For the first time in my life, I want someone, feel a tug to them like the Fates have woven a string around both our souls and tied them together. I want her so deeply that my body has given me no choice but to feel this need and desire all building up in ways I can barely comprehend. Sure, I've understood sex from a scientific stand-point and why the gods enjoy it. But now, only now, do I truly see.

This intimacy. This trust. We've yet to enough touch one another, and I feel a closeness to her that cannot be replicated.

When she cries "Than" again, she stills her fingers as her pussy contracts around them. Any worry is long gone from her face, any fear dissipated. The sight of her and the vulnerability of it all, vulnerability that she's sharing with *me* of all the gods, causes me to spill onto myself.

I'm aware of the whimper that passes my lips, but it sounds so unlike me that I don't immediately register it. My release hits me in shockwaves as my orgasm coats my hand. I'm able to catch most of it in my fist, leaving minimal mess, and I can't take my eyes off Seph.

We sit like this for a moment, panting and staring at one another. It's like a battle of the wills, both of us waiting to see if the other will back down first. As I scan her, I wonder if she thinks I'll disappear again. Part of me is tempted to, but I can't. Not after tonight. Another line has been crossed, one that should have been left well alone.

Instead, I surge forward and kiss her. She doesn't stop me, only leans into to press her lips further against mine. I support my weight with my free hand, hovering above her so only my cum-filled fist covered by my chitin separates us. My hair hangs over her like a curtain, and I hope it is enough to shield her from omniscient eyes and any harm that the Underworld may send our way. Our lips both part, our tongues both collide, and Seph tastes sweeter than any fruit she could have grown in the garden.

With this kiss, I have damned myself to an eternity of

always wanting more. I will never be able to get enough of her, and I try to consume her with my kiss as best as I can.

This can't happen again. I fear it will anyway. I hope it does. When I tell her as much against her mouth, she only says, "I know. Me too."

"I should go. We shouldn't push our luck."

"You're right. Please, Than. Don't disappear on me without warning anymore. Promise me."

Duty demands I tell her I cannot make such a promise. Yet that Fate-made string connecting my heart to her has me making that promise anyway.

CHAPTER 13
SEPH

Over the coming weeks, I don't see much of Thanatos. While his new reaping assistants grant him some time off, it doesn't allow him to slack off entirely. When a plague or a war happens on the surface, he's especially busy. Despite Ares handling the soldiers and perpetrators, Thanatos still tends to innocents caught in the crossfire.

He visits me whenever he has a spare moment. We don't dare speak of the night he caught me pleasuring myself to him, nor do we bring up how he joined me. There's no time. He flutters in, asks if I'm well, and is gone as soon as I answer. If I'm lucky, he leaves a chaste kiss on my cheek as he teleports away. The feeling of his lips on my skin lingers longer than he's here.

One day, he parts with a gift for me: a black swallowtail butterfly. Its wings, tipped with yellow and blue on the bottom, are the most beautiful I've ever seen. The butterfly perches itself on my robe where a brooch may go, then solidifies into solid adamant.

"So I may keep tabs on you. So long as you wear that, I'll be able to hear you. Call my name and I'll be there."

"Won't you need it?"

"I have others. Besides, you know this one."

As I realize it's the same butterfly from my death day, he's gone again in a poof of smoke and shadow.

The disaster happening on the surface grants me some respite, though. Hades is as busy as Thanatos is. I learn through the crisis that Hades's roll is, in a nutshell, handling punishments and paperwork. Most of the punishments are delegated to the Furies, or some other monsters under his control, and he only comes out to handle the worst of the worst.

I've taken advantage of my free time by training even more with the Furies. Down to two at a time now, what with the new flux of souls, but I become strong and handy with more weapons nonetheless. My whip technique is nowhere near as good as Megaera's, but it's passable. It grants me some form of agency, makes me feel empowered. When I'm not training, I'm in the archives, trying to find some way I can kill a god.

To kill The God of the Dead will be no easy task. Solutions don't present themselves to me, only snippets of ideas. But if anyone can do this, I can. I can think of no other reason or purpose for my being brought here, reincarnated, than this.

It goes on like this for months. I only know how long because Thanatos is able to glean the date on the surface during his visits. Eventually, it ends. When it's done, he finds me en route to my chambers from the training grounds.

"That should be the last of them," he says by way of greeting. "Are you well?"

"I am. Even more so now that you're back. You'll be staying a while, then?"

Thanatos nods. "Business as usual now. Not sure for how long, but I'll take what I can get."

"I've missed you."

"And I you. Can I ask you something, Seph?"

"Of course."

"It's rather embarrassing. But when I'm around you, I feel… something I can't name, at least not entirely. This feeling is foreign to me. And I need to know if this feeling is mutual, lest I go mad."

"How do you feel?"

"Tight. Right here, in my chest." He places a fist on his solar plexus. "And also in the pit of my stomach. It spreads down to my hips. And to other areas."

I suspect I know, but I want confirmation. "Where else, exactly?"

"Like I said, it's embarrassing."

"I won't judge you. Speak freely."

"You must forgive me, then." Thanatos gazes at the tile beneath our feet. "When I see you, especially in certain lights, I desire you in a way I've desired no one else. Like when I saw you that night. And like now."

He looks up at me, assessing my gaze. When he finds no malice or judgement, he clears his throat and continues.

"The torchlight, it catches your hair, and I can't help but wonder how it may look cascading down your bare skin. And then I wonder how soft your skin feels. I've never wondered that about anyone before, not in all my years. But I'm struggling with this attraction. Because when I look at you, I can't tell if I'm hopeful or if you feel that way, too. And you're consuming every one of my spare thoughts."

"You've never had a partner? Romantically, I mean. Or even sexually, no other strings attached?"

Thanatos shakes his head. "No. Not many would wish for the cold embrace of death. So I've never bothered. And perhaps it's because you're the first person who isn't a relative that I've become close to. That may have something to do with it. We've formed a kinship since you arrived, or so I'd like to think."

"It's a mutual feeling, Than. In every way." I drop my voice. "Otherwise, that night would've never happened."

A smile spreads across his face; he knows the one I mean. "Well, thank the darkness for that."

I glance both ways down the corridor, then take Thanatos by the hand. "Come with me."

"Where are we going?"

We take the few steps to my chambers, where I usher him inside. I check the hallway again before I close the door, relieved to have not spotted a single resident of the house.

"I shouldn't be here."

"I know you shouldn't. But you are. At my urging. Now, let me ask you. Did you want to stop wondering and take things further?"

"If he ever found out—"

"He won't. And I'm not his bride. He can't punish you." I squeeze his hand. "We can keep this between us, though. To play it safe."

"Then yes. I would very much like to stop wondering."

I guide his hand up to my shoulder, where one of the brooches holding my robe together is. Thanatos unfastens it, then the other, letting the garment fall to the floor. I'm not shy, especially not after the other night. He drinks me in nonetheless, soaking up every inch of me.

Thanatos swallows, then asks, "May I touch you?"

"I'd love nothing more. Come on. Let's get comfortable."

I remember how anxious I was my first time, and how comfort can make all the difference. Despite him being nearly as old as time itself, Thanatos has never done this before. Grateful that he trusts me enough for intimacy, I guide him to my bed. The mattress dips beneath our weight, and he follows me on.

As I sprawl out, lounging against the mountain of pillows, Thanatos asks, "Should I undress first?"

"Undress whenever you'd like, if at all. We can take things at your pace."

He nods, focused on my body. His hands start at my hips, then run up my sides. There's a sharp chill to his touch, but it's pleasant like I imagined it would be. "If something doesn't feel good, promise you'll tell me."

As soon as I promise, he cups my breasts. Fingertips ghost over my skin, and he notices the light sigh I can't help when his thumbs rub over my nipples. Thanatos repeats the motion a few times, sending a shiver down my spine, before exploring more of my body. He relishes every dip and curve, gripping where he can to feel how my body reacts to his touch. With knit together brows, I can tell he's focused as he finds the erogenous zones and soft parts.

"Feels wonderful, Than." I see his body relax at my praise.

"Can I kiss you?"

"Please."

He lowers himself onto me, pressing our lips together at last. Like the rest of him, his kiss is cold. But his lips are plush and soft, a sharp contrast to the hard lines and muscles of his body. I cup his face as we kiss, and Thanatos follows my lead until he feels more confident. When my tongue darts past my lips, he follows suit, meeting my passion with equal fervor.

Above me, I feel his cock hardening beneath his chiton. It presses against my thigh, and it's then that Thanatos breaks our kiss. Something about his erection feels unique, a hard, smooth ball at the tip. Perhaps it's his anatomy, or it's something else I'm not privy to beneath his robe. I'll find out soon enough.

I press my lips to Thanatos's neck, and he shudders above me. "It's okay, Than. May I touch you, too?"

Opal eyes blown wide with lust, he nods. "I think I'd like that."

"We can always stop."

"I don't want to stop. Quite the contrary."

My hand caresses his thigh. With his chiton only reaching the top of his knees, I have easy access to the space between his legs. And given the laissez-faire attitude everyone here has about nudity, no one bothers to wear undergarments.

I start with Thanatos's outer thigh, working my way up and in. He whimpers above me the higher up I inch, chest rising and falling rapidly. As I do, he mirrors the action on my own thigh until his hand finds my cunt.

"Go ahead, Than," I say against his skin. I kiss his neck, wanting to encourage him. "Your touch feels so good."

His fingers trace my lower lips, studying how they feel and my reactions once more. With my free hand, I guide him to my clit, showing him how to rub the way I like. Thanatos is a quick study, and the way my back arches must be reassurance enough, because he keeps at it. As I grow closer to my first climax, Thanatos pulls away.

"Are you alright?"

"I've entirely too many clothes on." He strips of his robe, and it's the first time I've seen him fully naked. Muscles ripple across his entire body, but he's not comically large. He reminds me of the statues I've seen in museums, which were all more accurate than I ever realized in showing forms like his.

Thanatos's cock stands hard and long, and I see the feature I failed to identify earlier. A silver piercing, the same shade as his scythe's blade, sits at the tip of his cock. The small ball is right beneath the opening, with a ring running along the topside of the tip.

Returning to bed, he kisses up my legs, covering as much of my skin with his lips as he can. When his fingers resume at my core, he finds my wetness there. His curiosity must be driving him, or perhaps its some greater instinct, because he dips a finger between.

I continue stroking his thigh, but now reach further up. I cup his balls first, and he groans at the mere touch. It's not long until my fingers wrap around his base, then glide along his shaft. Thanatos's cock twitches in my grasp, growing harder still. His hips thrust, and a better idea comes to my mind.

Pressing a hand against his chest, I flip us over. "Lean back," I instruct. "Let me take care of you."

CHAPTER 14

SEPH

Eyes blown wide with lust, Thanatos nods. I lower myself so I'm faced with his crotch, then rub my tongue along his shaft. One of his hands flies toward his mouth, where he bites down on a knuckle to stop himself from moaning too loud. The other reaches for my hair, tangling between my locks as I wrap my lips around him. He breathes through it as I bob my head up and down, pressing my tongue against his piercing for extra stimulation.

Around his knuckle, I hear him groan, "Fuck," drawing out the vowel. Everything about Thanatos right now—his bare form, his pierced cock in my mouth, how responsive he is—builds my own desire. "Slow down, lest we cut this short."

I lift my head, then straddle his waist without sinking down on him yet. "Do you want me to continue?"

He sits up. "Is that even a question?"

"Making sure."

"You're being careful for my sake. I appreciate that, but I'm not fragile. Just promise you'll take the lead for now."

"Like this?"

As I lower myself onto him completely, he chokes out a

moan. His long, dark hair—so black it's like looking at the night sky—hides his face like a veil, but I feel him rest his forehead against my shoulder. Cold breath hits my collarbone in short puffs as I rise and fall on him. I feel his piercing against the sweet spot within me, and it provides just the right amount of pressure to drive me mad. But I keep my cool for Thanatos, who unravels beneath me with soft whimpers—now muffled by him biting my shoulder.

"Does it feel good, Than?" I feel him nod. Stroking his hair back so I can see his face, I continue, "Is it too much?"

With a gasp, he says, "Yes. I— No. Gods, no. Don't stop. Please don't stop."

Beneath me, he trembles. So I keep stroking his hair as I ride him, taking things nice and slow so he doesn't get too over-whelmed. To gain better access to his ear, I brush a large section of it back over his shoulder. I kiss the spot on his neck right beneath his lobe, which is lined with small, silver rings that continue up to the top of his ear.

Whispering into his skin, I say, "It doesn't have to be today. But we can always go faster or slower or whatever pace you want. You can set the pace, too, from either below or above me."

Thanatos starts to rock his hips, trying to match my speed. It takes him a few thrusts, but eventually he ends up in sync with me so he moves up as I lower onto him. It's just enough for me to reach my peak, and his cock is thick enough that I feel nothing but Thanatos as I clench around him. Seeing him so full of trust and need beneath me fuels something in me, too, and it's just dawned on me that I'm not only fucking Death Incar-nate, but in control.

"There you go," I encourage. "Just like that."

His hands grip my sides tighter as he feels me come undone around him. "Gods. Not sure I'll last much longer."

"It's okay if you don't. Do you feel that? It means I've

enjoyed myself rather thoroughly. Anything after this is ambrosia."

The metaphor lands, understanding flashing in his eyes. With only a few more thrusts, Thanatos spills inside me. I slow my hips, but don't stop entirely, letting him ride out his orgasm. He leans up to kiss me, hard and messy but so fueled by passion that it leaves me dizzy. I don't still until Thanatos stops coming, and it's only then when he breaks our kiss. With heavy breaths, he presses our foreheads together and cups my face. Some of his hair sticks to his forehead, but I don't mind the faint tickle of it.

I ask, "How are you feeling?"

"More connected to you than I have been to anyone. Please tell me I'm not alone. That you feel this strongly for me, too."

"I do, Than. I do. We wouldn't be here if I didn't."

He sighs. "A relief. Can we stay here for a moment?"

"We can take all the time you need."

"You're so much softer than I imagined. And so warm. And not warm like it is when I return here from the surface. Something more comforting. Am I making any sense?"

"You are."

"And am I warm to you? Or, being who I am—what I am— do I feel different?"

I consider his words, thinking of the best way to answer while remaining honest. "Not warm, but still a comfort. You're cold to the touch, yes, but I've always liked the cold. And considering where we are, it's a welcome reprieve."

"Good. That's good." Thanatos kisses me again, gentler this time. Sweeter. "I don't want to withdraw, but I can't imagine this being very comfortable for you."

"I'm fine. Truly. We can stay like this as long as you need."

My cunt clenching around him seems to be enough reassurance for Thanatos, who groans. "Fuck, that's incredible. You're incredible."

"You do this to me. Only you."

As his fingers trace my spine, the only way I can describe his smile is love-struck. It's a sweet look, foreign on his face, but so beautiful and vulnerable that I wish I could capture it forever. No one's ever looked at me like this, let alone Death himself.

It should scare me. None of it does. Not in the slightest. I'm sure the look on my own face isn't much different.

I glimpse down at the mess between us, where his cum leaks out despite him still within me. There's so much, I'm not surprised. "May I ask what may be a stupid question?"

"Nothing you ask could be stupid. But yes. Go on."

"It's about contraception."

"A matter of divine will. As gods, we can choose the end result. I would never wish a child upon you without your first saying so. And given the circumstances we're in right now, I won't propose that any time soon. Pregnancy wouldn't help us keep this a secret, now would it?"

I sigh in relief. "That's good to hear."

"A lot of the gods use it to flex their power. But that's never been my style."

"For that, I'm eternally grateful."

"You deserve to feel safe, Seph. Especially after everything. Know that whatever it is you have planned, I believe in you. Your vision to make the Underworld a better place. I'll stand by you. You understand?"

"Thank you. We can talk about all that later." While I have a few ideas that I've brainstormed, there's nothing fully formed yet. There are others I need to speak with first. I brush back some of Thanatos's hair, then kiss his forehead. When I pull away, tears well in his eyes, giving the effect of a shimmering gemstone.

Thanatos takes a deep breath, staving off his tears. "My

apologies. No one's ever been so tender with me. So unafraid. And I..." His voice trails off. "I'm at a loss for words."

"You're overwhelmed. It's okay." I continue brushing his hair back, and he leans into my touch like he's been starved of it his entire immortal existence. "What do you need?"

"You. Just you."

"I'm here. I'm not going anywhere."

Thanatos kisses me deeply as he slowly withdraws at last. I feel the loss of him right away, clenching around him one last time on his way out, and then at the space he left behind.

"I've a private bath," I say against his lips, "adjoined to my chambers. We can clean ourselves up together, then stay in bed the rest of the night."

"And if he comes looking for you?"

"He won't. He's been too busy. We have the night to ourselves."

Thanatos hums in agreement as he nuzzles his nose into my shoulder. He leaves a few kisses behind before scooping me in his arms, carrying me to the bath. Once we're lowered into the water, Thanatos takes it upon himself to clean the space between my legs, then massages my thighs once we return to bed.

"I appreciate you being patient with me. Both tonight and in general. I know I haven't been the easiest to deal with."

"This is new territory for both of us."

An echo of the Thanatos the rest of the Underworld knows is still there. He's gone pensive, deathly quiet as he kneads with the sweet gentleness I've come to know.

I ask, "You okay?"

"I am. Sorry, little butterfly. Everything hit me all at once."

"Than, come here."

He works his way up my body, and I guide him to snuggle against me. A refreshing chill runs over my skin as we curl up to one another, Thanatos's head coming to use my breasts as a pillow. Our legs weave together like a braid, and Thanatos drapes his arm around my waist protectively.

"This can help if things get intense to relax like this after."

He hums in understanding. "This is nice."

I can't help but run my fingers through his hair, spotting some white streaks amongst the black like shooting stars streaming against the sky. In the afterglow, our silence is comfortable.

I almost think he's fallen asleep until he says, "I've never allowed myself to get close to anyone like this."

He doesn't just mean physically, I know.

"It's easier that way, to keep everyone at arm's length. To be uncaring. No one wants to die, so they want nothing to do with me. When mortals pray to me, it's not out of reverence, but fear-driven hope for a swift end. 'A job is a job,' I always told myself, 'and if they fear me, then so be it. I'll let them.' But *you*. You were never afraid of me. Not then. Not now."

Thanatos props his head up, looking me in the eyes now. Tears threaten to spill again, but he's holding them back. Even so, he's being so vulnerable that I can help but treasure this moment, feel it burrowing into my chest.

"Do you have any idea what that means to me? How lonely of an existence I've had? Even as a mortal, when I came for you, you did not weep or scream or fight. Sure, you were nervous, but you simply asked me if you could finish your book. Like I was a librarian and not the Grim Reaper. I'd never felt so normal in my entire life."

With a hint of teasing in my tone, I say, "It was a *really* good book."

He laughs, not the huffy breath he usually does, but truly laughs. It's the most beautiful sound I've ever heard, deep and light all at once.

"I mean it. Very steamy. I couldn't miss the couple's last kiss."

"I'd never sat with a mortal before. Never gave them an extra second, never mind few minutes. People have begged and pleaded, sure, but never so calmly just... asked the way you did."

"You never gave me a reason to fear you."

"Not even by nature of who I am?"

"Not even by that."

"I know it's customary for the gods to take as many lovers as they please. But I'm selfish, and I want you for myself. You're the only one I'll have."

I can't help but smile at him. It's all pouring out of him now, and I wonder how long this has all been bottled up, waiting for someone to unleash it. "Where I come from, monogamy is the norm. I'm yours, Than. Only yours."

Even if Hades tries standing in our way, there is no denying who my heart belongs to.

"Thank the darkness for that. You're sure I can stay?"

"I'd prefer if you did."

"Good." He settles into my bed, my body, every fiber of my being. I've never seen Thanatos so relaxed, and it seems he's worked through most of the emotions running through his head. Then, he asks a question I didn't anticipate: "Being this was my first time, did I do alright? You were satisfied?"

I kiss the top of his head. "Very much so, Than. You're a quick study."

"Here I am, rambling on about how special you are to me, and gods forbid you hated every second."

"I don't think I could ever hate a second spent with you."

"So when I felt you squeezing, almost, was that..?"

"Mhm."

"Ah. Now I know. It felt—*you* felt divine."

"We can try different positions and things to do next time.

Discover what you like the most. If you prefer to be more dominant or submissive."

"And which do you prefer?"

"I'm a bit of a switch. Some days, I like to be more in charge. Others, I wouldn't mind submitting to your whims."

"Oh!" His eyes widen a bit. "Well then. That leaves us lots of room to experiment, doesn't it?"

Thanatos leans up and kisses me before I can respond, moving his lips against mine in languid passion. His fingers dance along my exposed skin, trying to find more spots that make me whimper beneath him. When his cock twitches back into full hardness, he looks up at me from beneath his eyelids, eyes brighter than any gem, and asks if he can try entering me from on top this time.

I don't hesitate to spread my legs, to welcome him back into my cunt. Having him in me again feels like being home. Thanatos's hair hangs over us like a wall of shadow.

"Tell me what to do," Thanatos says. "Tell me how to make you feel good like this."

So I talk him through it, helping him adjust the angle or speed as we go. When I tell him he can throw my legs over his shoulders to go deeper, he tries it, groaning in pleasure with every thrust. The sounds—both from him and from where our bodies meet with each thrust—send my senses into overdrive. We go at it all night, a cycle of trying a position, cock-warming after, and then taking a break before our hands roam again.

We aren't sure how many nights we'll get like this, where we know Hades won't be a threat to us. We might as well take full advantage of it.

CHAPTER 15
THANATOS

I didn't realize I could be addicted to a person.

Until her.

We sneak away when we can. Sometimes it's to her chambers, other times to mine. If we know Hades is around, we don't risk it. But the next few weeks are spent with Seph teaching me how to please her.

And I've every intention to be a good student.

She tells me a name for how I feel. Demisexual: requiring an emotional bond before feeling attraction or arousal. While I'm not one to care what others think of me, it is nice to know that it's common enough for it to have a label. To not be the outcast among the Greek gods, known for fucking freely and frequently. Given I'd only started feeling how I do after developing a close friendship with her, I agree with the sexual alignment. I always found her beautiful, much like how one can find a painting to be a masterful work of art. But this desire is so different.

And acting on it with her only makes me feel closer to her.

Like now, as I cage her beneath me with my arms. The tip of my cock slides along her entrance. As my piercing nudges her clit, Seph whines, and it's delicious. Every sound she makes is sweeter than any nectar. Hades is tending to business in Tartarus, and I've returned mere moments ago from the surface, so we aren't worried about anyone suspecting us. I've taken to returning from jobs via her chambers.

So long as one of my butterflies is with her, I can teleport right to her. She keeps the one I gifted her on her robe at all times. She's taken to wearing more jewelry, too, so it blends in. No one suspects it's from me.

My thrusts are slow, yet rough. I caress Seph's jaw, then run my thumb along her chin. As it trails to her lips, she captures my thumb in her mouth, sucking on it like she would my cock. This earns her another thrust, and she moans against my finger. Every time I feel her tighten around me, it draws me deeper into her, wanting more.

Because no matter how much Hades wants her, we have one another. *She is mine*, I think, and I think it every time I sheathe myself in her. *Mine*. In a past life, he may have taken her, wed her. But now, she is mine.

Mine.

Such possession has never overcome me before. Perhaps it's because I've yet to have anyone or anything truly to myself.

I pump deeper into her, experimenting with a faster pace. Her head rolls back against the pillow, auburn hair splayed behind her in a bed of waves, and I lose myself to pleasure. To her.

Mine.

And who better for the maiden of spring, of life, to have has her own than Death?

My brother was right; it explains our connection. We're two sides of the same obol. While I'd never be so presumptuous as to assume what the Fates have in store, the signs all lead to this —to us—being meant to be.

Everything I touch withers and dies. Now, though, something blooms in my heart.

Hades seeks her out more with each passing day. This does not bode well for us. The days blur together, each one tightening the noose around our secret, each night growing shorter as his shadow stretches longer.

The corridors are quiet, but never for long. The palace practically lives and breathes in groans of drifting shades, the distant clatter of armored feet, of Hades and his workers and my reapers and gods know who else. I keep my ears sharp, each faint echo rolling through me like thunder. Because I'm not alone.

She's here in the dark hallway. Seph presses her back to the wall, eyes wide, breath coming quick. I know we should part, know the risk of a handmaiden, a Fury, or worse—him—appearing around the corner.

But she looks at me like I'm the only solid thing in a world built of smoke and mirrors, and I can't say no to her.

My hand finds Seph's waist, fingers curving into the folds of her gown. I pull her close, pressing her into the chill of the stone. Her breath hitches, lips parting as mine find hers. Our kiss is hungry, almost frantic, as if every time might be the last.

A torch crackles overhead. The shadows dance across her face, across mine. I taste the sweet pomegranate she ate earlier, and feel the heat of her sigh against my mouth.

"Someone will see," she whispers between kisses, voice trembling with nervous laughter.

"Then we'd better be quick." I catch her bottom lip between

my teeth before kissing her deeper. Her hands tangle in the folds of my cloak, pulling me closer until every inch of me aches with wanting.

Another footstep. This one closer. We break apart, breathless, but it's like we're two magnets refusing to separate. My thumb skims her cheek, chasing the flush I left behind.

"I don't want to stop," she murmurs.

"I'll never want to."

She lets out a shaky laugh, but it's short-lived. The footsteps draw nearer. I pull her deeper into the shadows, pressing her against the curve of an alcove. Her eyes shine up at me, wild and bright.

"Go," I whisper, voice low and harsh with need. "Before they find us."

She hesitates, fingers slipping from mine like a secret we're both terrified to name. "Meet me in the garden later." Then she darts down the hall, skirts whispering around her ankles. I watch until the dark swallows her up.

I'm left alone in the hush of the palace, mouth still burning with her taste. Knowing every stolen second makes the fall we're hurtling toward so much steeper.

She's already there when I arrive. Shadows lap at her skirts, dark green silk melting into midnight grass. The torchlight makes her hair look like a dark fire, and she appears more at home than she realizes. She's pacing, movements sharp, restless. A storm bottled in a body that should never have known fear.

When she sees me, she doesn't smile. She grabs my hand, pulling me into the shelter of an old willow. Its branches drape around us like a veil.

"We're running out of time," she says. Her voice isn't a tremor, but a blade. I have to admit, I admire her urgency. "If we're going to do something—if we're going to stop Hades and be together—we have to act fast."

I'm frozen, her words cracking through me like a bell toll.

"Seph..." I start, but she cuts me off.

"I've been reading everything," she says fiercely, eyes bright as the sky on a clear day. "There's a way to change how the Underworld works. To take control of the flows of death itself."

I exhale slowly, trying to make sense of what she's saying, but she's already moving—pulling a scroll from her cloak, unfurling it in the moonlight.

"Tell me," she demands, voice shaking with urgency. "Who decides where souls go? Who calls for a reaping?"

I hesitate. My instincts scream to stay silent—to keep her safe, to keep us hidden—but the look in her eyes won't let me lie.

"The Fates weave the threads," I say, hushed. "They set the span of life, the shape of death. But it's not only them. Hades makes his will known when the balance is threatened. He chooses when to send me, or to withhold me."

Seph glances at the scroll, which details how the Fates cut a life, then stares at me like she's peeling back every word. "So it's not just the Fates."

"No." I swallow hard, forcing myself to continue. "There's a third. The Queen of the Underworld. The power has always been hers, too. Equal. But..." My chest tightens. "You never used it. In your past life, that is."

She grins, scheming. "So I can?"

"Yes," I rasp. "If you claimed it."

Silence crashes over us, thick with the scent of damp earth and night-blooming flowers. I feel the heat of her hand in mine, the way her pulse flutters beneath my thumb. I must have kissed her at least hundred times now, but never felt this raw, this close to something irreversible.

122

"If I take it," she says softly, eyes locking on mine, "if I stand beside you, they'll know everything."

"Yes." I hate how the word trembles in my mouth, hate feeling so uncertain.

"They'll try to stop us."

"They will." I lean in, my forehead brushing hers.

She exhales shakily. "Then we have to be faster than them."

Her lips meet mine, fierce and claiming. To be wanted like this sets my cold skin alight. My hands fist in her hair, pulling her flush against me, the kiss bruising, desperate. The willow rustles around us, leaves whispering secrets to the sky.

When we break apart, her eyes burn with determination that terrifies and thrills me in equal measure. "Promise me," she says, voice low and dangerous. "When I move, you'll stand with me."

I press my mouth to hers again, softer this time, sealing the words against her lips. "Always."

And in that moment—firelight cutting through the dark, her heartbeat wild against mine—I know the tide has turned. Seph has some sort of plan. I just don't know what yet.

CHAPTER 16
SEPH

The next time I have a nightmare, I force myself awake. I need to talk to Melinoë, so I'm relieved for once to see the horrors she has in store for me. When I wake, I find her sitting at the edge of my bed, her dark curls tied up into a ponytail, bangs pulled back into braids.

"Mel, you're here."

She whips her head around to look at me. "Moth—Seph! I'm sorry. It wasn't too bad tonight, was it?"

"No. But I have a question for you."

"Ask me anything."

"Can you tap into my dreams to get me in touch with others? Perhaps those in Olympus? Does it work like that?"

Melinoë shakes her head. "I only have control of your nightmares. But Hypnos might be able to help. Can we trust him, though?"

I don't hesitate. "He's proven himself to me. Erebus and Nyx, too. Thanatos's whole family has."

She gapes at me. "Thanatos? The Death God?"

"And the first friend I made here, yes."

"Friend, or..?"

"The details of our relationship aren't appropriate for a mother to share with her daughter."

A knowing smirk graces Melinoë's face. It's almost frightening to see her smile, what with her void-like eyes. "Well. Here I was, only teasing. Now this is a development."

"And unimportant. You think Hypnos can do what we need?"

"If he can't, Hermes can. And they've been known to enjoy each other's company on more than one occasion."

"I don't want to include any more people than we need."

"Come on. We can go to Hypnos now, if you'd like. Like Thanatos, I can teleport. Helps me get from place to place faster, should I need to infect the masses." She says it as casually as one might mention what they ate for breakfast. Melinoë extends a hand to me. "Shall we?"

I take her hand, and in a blink, we're standing on the edge of the Lethe. The river winds through a cave, and Melinoë guides me along the rocks. A few feet away, I can see the dark blue River Cocytus, though the wailing is faint here.

"If your feet get wet, it's okay. A lot of shades think swimming in the Lethe is what makes you forget. You'd only lose minor, unimportant memories in that case. You need to swallow the water to forget the big things."

I remember the first dream I had, where Persephone—where I—gulped as much of the water down as I could as I floated along, dagger in heart. Did I drink to forget on purpose? What happened to poor Persephone to make me want to forget it all in my current life? I know Hades hurt her, hurt me, but just how bad?

What did he do? Dare I ask?

To take my mind off it, I ask, "How well do you know Hypnos?"

"Not well. We work together from time to time, though I

can't say we know each other on a personal level. Though most folks don't know me on a personal level, if at all."

"You don't have many friends down here, either?"

"No. That's the trouble being the stuff of nightmares, isn't it? I should talk to Thanatos. He'd probably understand."

"You two would get along. He's very stoic, but sweet on the inside. Don't tell him I told you so, I'm sure he'd hate to think I'm spoiling his reputation."

Melinoë laughs. It echoes off the cave walls. "Our little secret, don't you worry." She's silent for a moment, then says, "You know, I'm glad you came back the way you did. You were such a wonderful mother to me. But you're my friend now, and I think I like that even better. You do consider us friends, right?"

Her nerves are palpable. Had she been anyone else, had our history been any different, I might have run in terror. But Melinoë, the woman with a face so similar to mine and who does everything she can to help me, is not one I need fear.

"I do, Mel. I'm grateful for you."

We reach the doors of Hypnos's cave, carved from wood. He must have had them sent here to guard his little corner of the Underworld, and it's strange to think I'd once died here. That this is where Hypnos found me, kickstarting this whole mystery to begin with.

I knock five times on Hypnos's door, hoping he hears at least one. When Hypnos doesn't answer, I rub my butterfly pendant, and in an instant, Thanatos is by my side.

Thanatos places his hands on my shoulders as he appraises me, eyes wide with worry. "Seph? Is everything okay?" He doesn't even notice Melinoë.

"I'm fine, Than. Mel's with me. We're trying to reach your brother, but I think he's asleep." I nod my head toward Melinoë and add, "She knows. Not all the details. But she knows."

Melinoë chimes in, "I'd never betray my mother, Thanatos,

in this life or the next. You've nothing to worry about, I swear it."

He's tense as he studies Melinoë. "If Seph trust you, then so shall I. But if you do a single thing to harm her, it won't matter who you are."

"She's sent me my past in the form of dreams. I'm hoping Hypnos can get me in touch with some folks on Olympus. Particularly Demeter and Dionysus."

Thanatos blinks. "Demeter, I understand. But Dionysus?"

Melinoë gets it right away, though. "He's my brother."

"Pardon?"

"He once went by the name Zagreus. But much like our mother, he, too, reincarnated after his death."

Recognition flares in Thanatos's eyes. "Zagreus and I were friends. You mean to tell me he lives on?"

"As the God of Wine, yes. I've seen his nightmares. I don't have to lift a finger to make him dream them."

"I can get you inside." Thanatos reaches into a pouch hanging from his belt and retrieves a small key. With that, he opens the double doors. "Do you want me to come with you?"

"Only if you have time. If you have other matters to attend to, I'd understand."

"I can stay."

Hypnos's living quarters look how I expect them to. Blankets and throw pillows litter the space, and every surface is lined with something soft except for a table hosting a tea set. The God of Sleep himself is on a chaise lounge, sleeping with his legs and arms twisted in such a way that it couldn't possibly comfortable.

Thanatos smacks the edge of the chaise, right near Hypnos's ear. The thud startles Hypnos awake with a yelp. He flails, but once he straightens and sits up, the gray-skinned god runs his fingers through his short, curly hair.

"By the gods, Than, what was that about?"

"You have visitors. And you can't be sleeping all the time, you know."

"Visitors? Tell them to come back later."

"It's Seph and Melinoë."

"Oh! Well why didn't you lead with that?" Hypnos stands, finally. He walks with such grace that it almost looks like he's floating, especially since his purple robes sweet against the carpet and stone floor. "Let me get you some tea! I've mostly got chamomile, but Than's finally started joining me for a cup every once in a while, so I've got some fruit blends that he likes. Which would you prefer?"

"A fruit blend sounds lovely, Hypnos, thank you."

Melinoë says, "Chamomile for me, if it's no trouble."

"It's my favorite, too!" He beams at Melinoë, so bright and ecstatic that it makes her raise her brows. "Why didn't you ever tell me that, Melinoë? I'd have invited you over for a cup way sooner."

"You never asked."

"That's true. Then again, I'm often guilty of daydreaming and dozing off on the job." I notice Hypnos's eyes don't leave Melinoë the entire time he makes our tea, but he's done this so often that muscle memory kicks in and he doesn't spill a drop.

I sip the fruit tea he's made for me and savor the flavor. Pomegranate, mulberry, and white tea blend together for a sweet, slightly tart blend. Thanatos has a cup, too, and he eyes me from over the rim. His expression shifts when he lowers his mug, the stern facade making way for softened eyes and a relaxed jaw.

As Hypnos prepares chamomile for himself and Melinoë, Thanatos whispers, "I drink this because of you, you know. It reminds me of you."

"What?"

"The flavor. It tastes like the pomegranate seeds we shared in the garden. And it makes me think of you."

Hypnos butts in, "So! What can I do you for?"

"I need to get in touch with some folks on Olympus. My godly mother, Demeter, and Dionysus. Formerly known as Zagreus."

"So that's what happened to your son. Huh. Well! You're looking to do so in sleep, I take it? Or do we need to get Hermes to deliver a note?"

"If you can do it on your own, I'd prefer that."

"For what it's worth, I trust Hermes. I'll only be able to tap into their dream conscious if they're also asleep, and I can't guarantee that without him passing the message along."

Melinoë asks, "And how will we get in touch with Hermes?"

"Oh, easy. I've a direct line."

"And you know he'll come?"

Strutting across the cave, Hypnos winks at Melinoë. "Trust me. He'll show up." Hypnos doesn't bother to pick up the lyre, simply leaning down to strum it. Even without proper play, its music takes my breath away. "Last time, he was here in a minute. I wonder if he'll beat his record."

In a flash of light, Hermes stands before us. Compared to everyone I've met thus far down in the Underworld, Hermes seems to glow. His blond hair sits shaggy yet cropped atop his head, contrasting against his dark brown skin, reminding me of aboriginal Australians and Pacific Islanders. Equally as beautiful as all the other gods—even Hades, despite his cruel soul, is far from ugly—and with a smile just as charming. Dressed in a short tunic and winged shoes, he greets Hypnos with a quick kiss to each cheek.

"It's past your bedtime." Even his speech is fast. "Looking for company?"

"I've a job for you. Requires discretion. Can you keep a secret?"

"Of course I can. You're my best-kept one to date."

Hypnos swoons. "Oh, you. You know my brother already. But have you met the others?"

"I don't think I've had the pleasure." Hermes holds a hand out for my daughter to shake, his movements so fast that they blur. "Hermes, at your service."

Hypnos continues introducing everyone. "This is Melinoë, the goddess of nightmares. We work together sometimes. And her mother, Persephone. Though, these days, she goes by Seph."

Hermes shakes Melinoë's hand, then freezes when he sees me. "Persephone? Didn't she die, what, twenty-something years ago?"

"That's what everyone tells me." I shrug. "Mel's helping me get my memories back."

Hermes asks, "Does anyone else on Olympus know?"

I shake my head. "No. But I'd like to change that, and I need your help."

"It would be my pleasure. What's the situation?"

"Listen, I'm only trusting you because Hypnos says I can."

Thanatos chimes in, "And if anything happens that results in her getting hurt, I'll kill you myself. Understood, Hermes?"

Hermes holds both hands up in innocence. "Whoa! Yes. Of course. Understood. Fill me in."

"When I died, I drank from the River Lethe. I reincarnated into this body, and had no memory of my former life. Hades had me reaped early, but is disappointed I don't have my memories, and is trying to woo me. Except I don't want to be his wife." Unsure of how much details to share, I don't dare glance at Thanatos. "Regardless of where my affections lie, the memories I've regained aren't exactly happy ones. Hades abused me, I think, in my past life. And in this one, I've seen some injustices in the Underworld that don't sit right with me."

Hermes whistles. "Wow. Well, I'm glad you're back with us, for what it's worth. We used to be friends."

"Did we? I'm sorry I don't remember you."

Hermes waves a hand in dismissal. "I'm not gonna fault you for that. When Hades kidnapped you the first time, your mother would have me send you messages. You'd send some back to her, too. We got to know each other through that."

"It's true," Melinoë adds. "I remember you telling me about that."

This adds to my trust. "I need to get a message to my mother again. And to Dionysus. I'd like to speak to both of them at the same time, if possible. My original thought was to do so through a dream, but Hypnos needs them to both be asleep for that, too."

"The fastest way about this will be for me to return to Olympus and tell them to get some rest immediately. Urgent message."

"I like the sound of that. Thank you, Hermes. Does that work for you, Hypnos?"

"Oh, yeah! Get comfortable. Hermes, let me know when they've gone to bed. I can help urge them along from here, and then we can all tap in."

"I'll be back in a jiffy."

He's gone in a blink, and in another, I am fast asleep.

Looking at Demeter is like looking into a mirror into my future. While I'll never age again, not unless I want to, I get a glimpse of what I may have looked like in forty years. Some white streaks her hair, but it still holds its dark brown and red highlights. The only differences in our faces are a few fine lines on her face and our eye color. Hers are a rich green, the color of grass on a summer's day. My blue must be Zeus's eyes, then.

Demeter rushes forward to me, her ice blue robes whirling around her as she does. "Is it true? My *kore* returns? Or is this some twisted dream that Hypnos has deigned to taunt me with?"

"No, no. Reincarnated as another woman named Persephone, but I'm your daughter, yes. My friends call me Seph. And you can call me Kore, if that was your nickname for me. But if it feels weird, Seph is fine."

Kore: Greek for 'girl,' said with a mother's adoration in this instance.

"My *kore*." Tears spill, not wasting a second as she holds my face in her hands. "I thought you lost to me for good. And to think! You even reincarnated with the same face and name."

When she embraces me, I can feel how much she loves me and has worried over the last few decades. I feel an instant connection with her, probably because the maternal instincts all but radiate off her. Any question of her nature is gone. So many tales paint Demeter as overbearing or strict, but they've got her all wrong. This is a woman full of grief and love all wrapped together.

In a wine-red robe, Dionysus appears next. Unlike me, he reincarnated with a face all his own, not that of his predecessor. He looks neither like me nor Hades, with sad, sunken eyes the color of red grapes and hints of the same shade in his black hair. Though his skin is perfectly sun-kissed, there's a dullness to it.

"Who the—wait. Demeter, is this..?"

My godly mother nods. "She's back. In a new body, but she's back."

Dionysus scratches behind his head. "So I guess that makes you my mom, sort of."

"Sort of. You don't have to call me that or anything. Just 'Seph' is fine. I'm glad you both came."

"We don't take sleeping summons from Hermes and Hypnos lightly," Demeter says. "And I'm sure you wanted to speak to us about more than your arrival."

"Yes. I need both of your help and advice."

"Anything." Dionysus smiles, even though it doesn't reach his eyes. "After everything the Greeks did to me, I've no love for them, save for you two. Whatever you need, Seph, count me in."

"So Orpheus got it right, then?"

Dionysus nods. "I drink to forget. It only kind of works."

Demeter frowns, then says, "What do you need, my *kore*?"

I explain my history to them, then say, "What I need to know is the politics of it all. How does it work with reincarnation? Even though I died, am I still technically the Queen of the Underworld? Or do I need to remarry Hades for that?"

"No, no. Your soul shall always be the Underworld's Queen, *kore*. You shan't need to marry him a second time if that's not what you want."

"Do you think Hades was trying to make this happen?" Dionysus adds, "After all, you can't return to the surface anymore."

"I suspect so. Word around the Underworld is the original Persephone died either by suicide or an unsolved murder. Maybe you're right and he tried to trap me, given my early reaping."

Demeter fidgets with some rings on her fingers. "I wouldn't put it past the old bastard."

"I need to kill him."

Dionysus laughs. "Oh, now this is a party!"

Demeter asks, "You think you can?"

"I killed once as a mortal. No one ever found out. Nemesis pardoned me and everything. If I could do it as a mortal, I can do it now."

"Adamant can kill us," Demeter says, "but to kill Hades, you'll need to be sneaky."

Dionysus waves his hand, procuring a bottle of nectar. "Take this. In case you need to resort to poison or anything."

"You can give me things in the dream realm?"

"We're gods, Seph. We can do whatever the fuck we want."

I take the bottle, its liquid contents reminding me of amber or honey.

Demeter adds, "Don't forget. As Queen of the Underworld, you hold the same authority as Hades down there. Promise me you'll remember that."

I nod. "Thank you both. I hope we can meet again, even if it's only like this."

"Me too, my *kore*."

"I like the new Persephone." Dionysus's grin lights his face up a bit more this time. "Call us again any time."

When I emerge from sleep, I find the bottle of nectar in my hand.

CHAPTER 17

SEPH

When I hear Hades is looking for me, I flee. Tartarus is better than this, though I find myself in Asphodel Meadows. It's dreary, all gray everything. No life touches this place, so I decide to experiment with my godly powers.

I will flowers to sprout at my feet, and I'm delighted when they do. It brings some life into this drab corner of the Underworld. The shades here may not be heroes or legends like those in Elysium, but they're not bad folks, either. They deserve a little cheer.

On my walk, I hear a man playing a lyre. His strumming is so sensational I can't help but stop, forgetting I'm running from Hades with my exploring in the first place. His voice is angelic, too, not singing any words but non-lexical sounds. I sit on the rock next to him, and he doesn't bid me go. Instead, he bows his head in acknowledgement and continues playing.

I suspect I know who this man is, with his long brown ringlet curls and sad brown eyes. His golden skin must have once held so much lustre. But when he's between songs, I ask anyway, "What's your name?"

"Orpheus, Your Majesty. Do you remember me?"

I know *of* him, yes. Who doesn't know Orpheus? Part of me wishes I could remember him, and I make a mental note to ask Hypnos to restore this to me in a dream: listening to Orpheus sing to us in court as he begged to bring Eurydice home. If my once-daughter can do this for me with my nightmares, I don't see why Hypnos can't achieve the same.

I tell him, "No, I'm sorry to say. My memory's all screwy. With a voice like yours, I wish I remembered hearing you play. But I've heard of you. Your legends are famous on the surface to this day."

He perks up a bit at that, how I imagine an abused dog might still perk up when offered a treat. "Wait, really? How long's it been? Since I passed, that is."

"So long that scholars debate if you existed or were part of the larger myth. But everyone knows your name. I'd reckon you're the most famous bard to date, if not one of the most. Where's Eurydice?"

His expression drops once more. "The Fields. I miss her. I miss her so, so much. Forgive me, Your Majesty. I should not trouble you with my woes."

I remember what Demeter told me about my power. "There's nothing to forgive. Eurydice is in Elysium? Then to the Fields you go. An artist shouldn't be kept from his muse and wife."

His brows lift. "Your Majesty! Do you jest?"

"About love? No, I would never. That would be cruel. I will this so, if you'd like."

He takes the strap on his lyre and shifts it, letting the instrument rest across his back like a guitar. "To what end do I deserve this kindness?"

"You never deserved this torment, Orpheus. Now, are you coming with me to Elysium or not?"

The lad hugs me, then catches himself and steps back. "I'm so sorry."

"It's okay, Orpheus. You must be so excited. It's only natural. You're not in trouble. Not so long as I'm here, okay?"

"What can I do to thank you?"

"Sing me another song. Does that seem fair to you?"

"Hardly, though I'm afraid it's all I have to offer anyhow."

We walk together toward the gate separating the realms. Orpheus plays the lyre the whole way and sings along with some of his original myths, melodies so beautiful I don't think anything I've ever heard can compare. Given his humility, I don't think he understands how much of a gift this is to me, to hear the original myths sung from Orpheus himself. It makes me wish I could go back in time, to tell my former self that she was right, that her college professor was wrong about Orpheus not being real.

When Orpheus breaks, I ask, "Why were you separated from Eurydice in the first place?"

"The judges wanted me to go with her. But Lord Hades was furious, you see, that I attempted to defy him. No one could justify my being sent to Tartarus, so I ended up here."

More injustices. I wondered how some other names I might know fared. Where did Odysseus and Penelope wind up, or Patroclus and Achilles? Were they split, too, by the whim of a god angry that his own wife hated him?

When we reach the gate to Elysian Fields, the shades tasked with guarding it let me right through. I let them know Orpheus is with me, and by order of the Queen he's getting an upgrade. They don't so much as bat an eye.

"May I ask what may be a personal question?"

"Of course, Your Majesty."

I don't ever correct him with the title. I need to get used to it, especially if I'm to tackle Hades. The Lord of the Underworld's downfall means one thing: I will be the ruler of this place.

"Why did you look back? Everyone has their theories. It's highly debated. I'd love to hear it from the source."

"The walk back was unlike anything I'd ever experienced. Torture, pure torture. I couldn't hear her footsteps. Nor her breathing, or her voice, or anything. All I could hear was the pained wails of the shades we passed by. And at the end, when I reached the surface, I was so eager to see her, so desperate and anxious and unsure if she made it, that I turned around too soon. I looked back because I loved her too much." He frowns. "I can only pray she'll forgive me."

"I'm sure she will."

When we find her, Orpheus stops in his tracks. Surrounded by fruit trees and flowers, Eurydice is as stunning as the songs make her out to be. As a nymph, her skin resembles tree bark more than flesh, and her hair reminds me of flourishing vines. Orpheus calls to her, and when she turns, her face lights up in a smile.

As they embrace, it's clear that all is forgiven.

As I watch them, my fingers subconsciously graze against my butterfly brooch. I don't even realize I've done such a thing until Thanatos arrives in a cloud of smoke.

"Everything alright?"

"Oh! Than. I'm so sorry. Everything's fine. I didn't even realize. Lost in a daydream." I nod my head to Orpheus and Eurydice. "My good deed for the day."

Thanatos doesn't smile in public, but he lets one corner of his lips twitch up. "A wonderful sight, to see them reunited."

I drop my voice to a whisper. "I think they reminded me of us. Forced to be apart."

"Why do you think we never realized this before?" Before I died, he meant. The unspoken words.

"I think my soul needed to be reborn first. I think I needed to experience everything I did in both lives for that thread to weave together. Besides, I don't see you as the type to even consider a married person as a possibility."

"You know me well. What brings you this way, anyhow?"

"Oh, Hades was looking for me so I snuck out. Took a stroll through Tartarus into Asphodel Meadows, where I found Orpheus playing his lyre. When he told me how he ended up there, I couldn't not do anything. My first royal decree."

"And a good one at that. I'm proud of you."

"Were you busy?"

"No. Just wrapping up. Perfect timing. Want company?"

"I'd love it. Show me around? This is my first time in Elysium."

Before Than can respond, Orpheus and Eurydice—who've finally broken from their embrace—turn to me. "Your Majesty!" Orpheus rushes forward with Eurydice, hand in hand. "We cannot thank you enough."

Eurydice then nods at Thanatos in respect. "Lord Death, honored to be here beside you."

"Don't worry," Thanatos says, his dry tone not revealing his real reason for being here. "I'm not here to split you up. My butterflies tell me everything." He lifts his finger, and one flutters over from one of the trees. "Was hoping I'd catch a duet, but I'm too early."

Eurydice giggles. "That can be arranged! It's been too long since we played together."

If Orpheus alone sounded angelic, it's like being transported to Heaven when he's joined by Eurydice. Other souls gather round, and no one questions why I'm here with Thanatos. Given his role, everyone must suspect we're simply coworkers doing our jobs. Before we leave, I initiate the hug with Orpheus, pulling Eurydice in, too. They both squeeze, and

I can tell they've needed it. Needed this, to be in one another's arms again and to sing each other's songs.

It gives me hope that this can be me and Thanatos one day.

The air in Elysium is so sweet it almost makes me dizzy. Soft grass sits cool beneath my knees, the quiet rustle of leaves are overhead, and I hear a distant stream threading through silver-lit meadows—one of the many rivers here, most likely. The stars shine brighter here, unclouded by the gloom of the palace. They catch on Thanatos' hair, turning him to something even more otherworldly than he already is.

His back is pressed hard against the rough bark of an oak. As I trail kisses down from his chest, his breath comes fast, chest rising and falling beneath the black silk of his robes. My hands splay over his ribs, feeling tension radiating off him. He looks down at me like I'm a storm about to break him.

His hands fist in my hair, hips canting forward as if he can't help it. I feel him trembling under me, and the power of it makes my own pulse thunder.

"Seph." He groans, voice shredded, breaking the quiet so perfectly it makes me shiver. I kiss down his torso, slow, savoring every inch of cool skin, tasting the faint sweetness of Elysian air on him.

My hands drift lower, slipping beneath his chiton to trace the lean, hard lines of his thighs. Without undoing the garment entirely, I push it aside, exposing more of his skin to me. His muscles jump under my lips as I kiss a trail down his stomach, tongue flicking along the hollow of his navel. His breath grows harsher, every exhale shaking him to his bones.

I press kisses lower still, lips ghosting the edge of his hip. His head tips back against the tree as a raw sound tears from his throat. His grip in my hair tightens almost painfully, but I love the sensation. It makes me feel alive.

And then Thanatos freezes.

His entire body goes rigid beneath my hands. His breath stops.

"Seph," he whispers, voice low and sharp as a scythe. His eyes flick to something over my shoulder, widening in horror. He adjusts his chiton in a flash. "Hide."

Before I can move, dense shadow explodes around me. The night becomes a living shroud, a cocoon of darkness thick with the smell of oak and lavender. Even though I've never been within the shadows that Thanatos calls home, it feels familiar. Like a comforting embrace after a long day, like I'm safe and swaddled in a blanket. I'm still fully aware of everything outside, so when I hear Thanatos instruct me to wave my hand, I do. He confirms that even he can't see me, so we're surely safe from Hades.

Just as the shadow rises up to his waist, I hear the god's booming baritone.

"Thanatos. I'm surprised to see you here. What brings you to Elysium?"

My lover straightens against the tree, and says, "From time to time, I check on the shades while my reapers tend to the new souls. Remind them that we're watching."

Hades accepts this answer. "Ah. Good to flex our power."

Thanatos swallows, and I see the muscle tension in his strong thighs within the shadows. His cock is stiff, protruding from his chiton, and I'm grateful for the shroud.

A darker part of me thinks it might not be so bad, though, if Hades were to catch us like this. If he could see Thanatos's hard member, right at eye-level with me, tempting me with how close he is. It'd be so easy to list his robe and wrap my lips around him, to lean forward and send him to the edge.

What would Hades do? Would he dare attack Thanatos, of all people, in front of all these shades? I doubt it. I'm not about to test that theory, but the thought alone of sucking Thanatos off with Hades mere inches away is enough to shoot desire straight to my core.

I don't want to distract Thanatos too much, so when he tenses further, I press my lips to his thigh. Thanatos responds by placing a hand in my hair, his fingertips all but grazing my scalp. His palm is flat against the top of my head, freezing me in place. When I kiss his thigh again, the muscle twitches, and I feel his thumb rub against my head in warning.

But Thanatos keeps his cool as he talks to Hades, and I dare not risk compromising us. After everything, I don't want to see him hurt, even if I'm starting to think Hades is all bark and no bite when it comes to anyone he can't control.

"Why the shadows?"

"Better to sneak around, don't you think? Especially at the edge of the meadow like this. All these trees make it so I can really blend in with them swirling about."

When I rest my forehead against Thanatos's leg, his grip loosens, but doesn't release on my hair. It doesn't hurt, and I trust him enough; he knows his strength, and doesn't have it in him to hurt me.

Hades asks, "Have you seen Persephone? She ran off. I've been searching everywhere, but she's either hiding well or on the move."

"I have not. If I catch her as I jump between shadows, I'll let you know."

"Most appreciated. She's to be sent home at once."

"Understood."

Hades steps away, then stops. From over his shoulder, he

says, "You've been visiting The Garden of Pomegranates. Tell me why."

"I've visited a few times since it reopened. Was curious enough to see the marvel myself. Quite the little miracle she pulled off, given the land was dead for almost thirty years."

"I didn't realize gardening was an interest of yours."

Thanatos shrugs a shoulder. "Not particularly. But the goings on of the palace are just as much my business as they are yours." He says it with no challenge or threat in his tone, only a matter-of-fact boredom. There is no way for Hades to misinterpret it as a challenge.

Whatever Hades is feeling, he doesn't show it. "That is true. I'll leave you to it, then. I've a bride to look for."

Hades teleports away, but Thanatos doesn't drop the shadows. He only clears them at the top of the cloud so he can see me.

"Are you out of your mind?" There's no anger in his voice as he asks it, not truly. I kiss his thigh in response, so close to his balls that he groans. "I can't be mad at you. Not when you're making me feel like this."

His cock twitches by my face, so I brush back his chiton to expose it to the shadows. The only thing colder than his skin is the chill of the piercing. Thanatos groans in pleasure as I run my tongue along the underside of his shaft, then wrap my lips around the tip right past the piercing. Thanatos's toes curl in his sandals, and he grips my hair tighter.

"Gods, Seph."

Part of me wants him to fuck my face. Because I know that Thanatos would never degrade me, would do so with as much respect as he could muster, and I relish in the moments where he takes control and comes into his sexuality. I continue my ministrations as normal, but just as his thighs begin to tremble, I slow down and leave my lips by the tip.

Thanatos looks down at me, eyes half-lidded with lust. "Are you alright?"

"Don't you think I need to be punished for teasing you earlier?"

"Punished? Seph, I... Oh. Oh, I see what you're saying. You want me to take control, is that it?"

I kiss his piercing. "I trust you to."

Thanatos adjusts his grip on my hair, holding it back into a ponytail with his fist. "Tap my leg three times if it's too much, okay?"

And then he thrusts into my mouth. He fills my mouth, guiding me up and down by my hair. The tug against my scalp is gentle, so I can tell he's holding back, not daring to use his full strength. I grip his thighs for extra stability, though I don't dare look anywhere other than right at his face.

CHAPTER 18

THANATOS

Seph looks up at me with those wide, blue doe eyes of hers and I nearly cum in her mouth from the sight alone. Her lips are bright pink, soft, and swollen around my cock, slick with her saliva as I dictate the speed. I start slow, not wanting to overwhelm her or myself. The idea alone of hurting her makes me queasy, but she trusts me so wholly and explicitly. I'll do everything in my power to prove I deserve it.

When her tongue dances along the spot right beneath my tip, extra pleasure shoots through my body. There's a mix of pressure, suction, and gentle stroking as I bob her head along, and her mouth is so wet and warm my eyes feel like they might roll into the back of my head.

But I can't stop looking at her. Not as my cock disappears into her mouth, not as she looks up at me with what must be love in her eyes, not as her nails dig into my thighs. I hope her fingertips leave marks, a sign that she's been there that only we'll see.

When I move slow for too long, Seph relaxes her tongue so I barely feel it. She's goading me on, trying to get me to unleash more power, so I give her what I want. I pick up the pace, tuning out everything around us: the flowers that keep blooming around her knees, the trees of Elysium, the bark at my back. It's just me, her, and my shadows.

I've touched a thousand souls, carried them across the boundary of life and death. I know what it is to watch the light leave someone's eyes, to feel the silence after a final breath. I thought I understood what it meant to take someone completely.

I knew nothing.

This isn't the quiet cold of reaping. It's a fire I can't smother, a heat that burns me from the inside out. She's soft and fierce, open and demanding even with me in control, and I find myself helpless against her—desperate to feel every sound she makes as it reverberates against my cock, to memorize every quiver of her lips around it.

I extend the shroud to cover me, too, not wanting anyone to see me as I bite my knuckle. If I don't, every shade will hear my moan as the back of my head hits the tree. While I feel my hair tangling in some loose bark, I don't care. Not as one of Seph's hands moves to cup my balls, squeezing ever-so-gently, making me groan again against my finger. As the ridges on the roof of her mouth run along the top of my length, her saliva pools at the corners of her lips and drips down her chin.

I want to ruin her for anyone else and to protect her so completely no one could ever touch her again. I want to give her everything I am, even the pieces I've never shown a soul. Every time she moans against my dick, it's a curse that we will both pay for this, that there is no way out of what we've started.

Because I know what this is. This isn't just lust, or hunger, or loneliness at its end. This moment is mine. She is mine, the possessive tendril wrapping around me once again. I let my shadows graze her body, wanting her to feel some sort of pleasure, too. As they caress the spot between her thighs, I glance further down and find she's toying with herself, already slick with her own want.

She's getting off to getting me off, and the implication behind that cleaves me open.

And when we come together, it's not two bodies, but two flames colliding in the dark, too bright to last, too perfect to ever let go. Somewhere in the rushing blood, in the heat and the whispered names, there's a terror I can't outrun—because I know what happens when the Lord of the Dead finds something precious slipping from his grasp.

But even if the Underworld cracks open beneath us, I swear I will never regret this.

Not a single moment.

Seph swallows every last drop, leaving no evidence of what we've done.

As she stands, her knees wobble, so I help her up. The world is silent but alive: a gentle breeze carrying the scent of wildflowers, the low murmur of the river beyond the tree line, the distant laughter of souls who have long since found their peace. I've never belonged here. I've always been the shadow on paradise's edge. But with her pressed against me, I could almost believe I do.

Almost.

She shifts her stance to lean against me, and the soft caress of her breath against my throat makes me shudder. I trail my fingers through her hair, marveling at its softness, memorizing how her warmth seeps into me like dawn driving back the night. I want to stay like this forever. But time is already slipping, each heartbeat a reminder that forever was never ours to claim.

She tilts her head to look up at me, eyes drowsy, luminous, searching. "Do you regret it?" she asks, voice husky from our kisses, from the way I fucked her mouth.

I don't hesitate. "No," I whisper, brushing my thumb over her cheek. "Never."

But the word tastes like a lie in my mouth. Not because I regret her, but because I know what this means. What it will cost. How many pieces of us we'll have to break off and burn just to survive the tempest coming for us.

Seph must read it in my eyes, because her lips press into a thin, trembling line. "I don't want to go back," she says softly. Her hand slides up, fingers curling around the nape of my neck, pulling me down until our foreheads touch. "Not yet."

"Then we won't." My heart slams at the recklessness of it. "We stay until the sunrise. Until the Furies come looking for us. Until he himself drags us back." We can't, and we both know it, but it's a wonderful fantasy.

She indulges me and laughs a fragile sound that still lights something inside me. I kiss her again, slow, lingering, tasting the salt of tears she won't let fall and my own arousal still on her tongue. She clings to me, her nails biting into my skin, as if she could keep me here forever by sheer will alone. We stay here in comfortable silence, holding one another as we come down from our shared high.

Around us, Elysium glows: golden mist dancing in the early morning light, flowers swaying in a breeze scented with memory and myth. For a heartbeat, it feels like we are the only two souls who have ever existed. Like the world was made for this one perfect, impossible moment.

But the light is already shifting. The wind grows warmer, thick with heat from deeper below. The birdsong fades. I know what's coming. I can feel it in the pit of my stomach, dark and heavy as the River Styx.

So I hold her tighter. I press every piece of my heart into the kiss I leave at her temple. And I promise myself: if this is the only peace we ever have, I will make it enough, because I don't know how many dawns like this we'll ever see again.

CHAPTER 19

THANATOS

The lounge is empty tonight. With Hades in Asphodel Meadows, forcing Seph to go along with him, this is one of our few chances for the rest of us to meet.

I stand by the hearth, fingers curled around the carved edge of the mantle. The heat of the fire does nothing for me, but it gives the illusion of a comforting warmth, and tonight, illusions are all we have. My reflection stares back at me from the brass kettle resting above the flames. My eyes are tired, and my mouth is drawn tight.

I hear the first set of footsteps: light, predatory. The Furies enter together, moving like a three-headed serpent. Megaera's eyes glitter cold, Alecto's smirk is a razor's edge, and Tisiphone's gaze flicks wildly between shadows as if searching for something to kill. They take their places without a word, leather armor creaking softly in the hush. One of the snakes in Megaera's hair slithers toward me, unable to leave her scalp but close enough to nudge my cheek with its snout.

"Hello to you, too."

It flicks its tongue out then retreats.

A softer sound follows: slippers brushing the floor. Hypnos

wanders in next, yawning so wide it looks like his jaw might unhinge. His eyes flick to me, warm but worried, before he curls into a high-backed chair that dwarfs his slight frame. Our mother follows him, greeting me with a kiss to each cheek before taking a seat for herself near the hearth.

A steaming cup of lavender tea appears in Hypnos's hands. It's the only flavor he drinks other than chamomile, saved for when he's nervous. Without either of us saying anything, he summons a second cup and passes it to me. I recognize it by color and smell alone: the pomegranate tea I've grown fond of. With a nod of thanks, I accept and sip. We've come a long way, my brother and I. And after all this, I owe him.

Last is Melinoë. She moves like mist, the pale half of her hair drifting around her sharp, thoughtful face. Her robes swirl behind her in gauzy layers of midnight as she closes the door behind her. She leans against it, arms crossed over her chest, eyes dark and measuring.

They all look to me. I straighten, pushing back the exhaustion pulling at my bones. The fire snaps.

"Thank you for coming," I say, my voice low but steady. "We don't have long. He's been more attentive lately."

Megaera raises an eyebrow. "How bad is it?"

"Worse than before," I admit, letting the words settle over us.

Melinoë glances at the hearth, firelight dancing across the sharp planes of her face. "Then let's not waste time."

They gather around the obsidian table, chairs scraping the stone floor. The Furies share looks that are more code than conversation. Hypnos cradles his tea, eyes flicking nervously between the others. Melinoë sets a dagger on the table, its curved blade catching the fire's reflection. I recognize it: it's the adamant one Hades used to kill Persephone.

"Got it while he slept."

I lean forward, palms braced on the cool stone. Their eyes fix on me. The harbinger of death, and now, the participant of a secret that could break the Underworld itself.

And for a moment, in the crackling silence, I wonder if we're already too late.

Megaera leans back in her chair, one boot propped on the table's edge. "You called us here because she's remembering things, isn't it?" Her eyes glint in the firelight, a hunter's gaze. "Or starting to."

Melinoë explains how she's provided the nightmare-memories over the last few months.

Alecto snorts when Melinoë is done, her fingers drumming on the hilt of her curved dagger at her belt. "And what would you have us do? Help her shatter herself? Or help Hades keep her blind and docile?"

Tisiphone hums to herself, eyes wide and unfocused. "Blood," she murmurs softly. "There will be blood if she awakens. There always is."

The words crackle in the hush. The flames sputter as if in protest.

Melinoë's voice cuts through the tension like ice. "Is it better to keep her ignorant, knowing how it will eat her alive?" She shifts her gaze to me, dark and unflinching. "Or how it will eat you alive."

My mouth goes dry. The question hangs heavy in the room, heavier than the scent of ash and fear. I want to tell them what it felt like to hold her, to taste the terror and hope in her kiss, to feel the truth of us thrumming beneath her skin. But I can't. Not yet. Even here, among those who might help us, words like that would damn us all.

Thankfully, I don't need to answer right away, because Hypnos says, "It's better if she doesn't know. There is no sense in traumatizing her a second time."

Megaera shakes her head. "As if being brought here before her time wasn't traumatizing enough as it was."

Hypnos gestures to me. "Hardly. Not with the way she and my brother get on."

I scoff. "That's beside the point. I grant all I visit a gentle death. That doesn't mean it isn't death, nonetheless. Mortals don't view it like we do. The unknown, it frightens them."

"If she is being pursued by the Master of the Palace," Nyx says, steering the conversation back on track, "then she deserves to know exactly what it is she's getting into. What his intentions are. Their history."

"But Mother," Hypnos leans forward, "she's no intention of being with him. Her lack of memory means she has no love for him. Best to let sleeping dogs lie."

Our mother turns to me. "You've been awful quiet, my son. You know her best. What do you think?"

"I think there's no sense in trying to decide for her. They're her memories. We can warn her of what she'll see. That way, she doesn't go in blind. And given what Melinoë has already fed her, I think she's got an idea for what to expect. But it should be Seph's decision."

I hear the door open behind me. "What should be my decision?"

Melinoë rushes to Seph, her robes billowing around her so it appears she's floating on a black cloud. "You're back early." As soon as the door is closed, she reaches for Seph, her hands resting delicately on the back of her biceps. "Are you okay?"

Seph embraces Melinoë. I notice my black swallowtail butterfly still perched on her shoulder. While she has the brooch, I wanted a live one with her just in case. A second set of eyes.

She answers, "I feigned exhaustion after traversing the Meadows with him all day. He believed me. Don't worry, I'm fine, and he didn't touch me. I swear it. He's on his way to Elysium. We have the place to ourselves still."

When Melinoë still evaluates her, I say, "My butterfly would have told me if she was in danger. Come in, Seph. We were discussing the matter of your memories. That is, if we should restore them in full or not."

"I'd like to get them back. I feel at a disadvantage when we speak."

"They're going to be unpleasant," Melinoë warns. "Even more so than what I've shown you so far. The things that were done to you..." She stops herself. "Unspeakable."

"I know. I know the stories. But I'll have you all." Seph locks eyes with me, and I nod once. "We'll get through this."

Megaera asks, "What do you wish to do after the fact?"

"We need to get rid of him. Permanently."

"Can we do that?"

"We can find a way. Perhaps my old memories will give us some answers. A clue, a weakness, anything." She looks at me and says, "Will you stay with me? When the memories return, that is."

"Of course. And perhaps my brother would be so kind as to ensure that, despite the horrors to come, you'll still rest well through it all."

Hypnos is mid-yawn. "Consider it done!"

My butterfly flutters from her shoulder back to me. Tisiphone, who's been notably quiet, places her hands on the table. "What's your relationship, exactly? Don't get me wrong, I'm still on board. But if we're going up against the Master of the Palace, I want to know what we're fighting for."

Alecto answers before either of us can. "Thanatos is too good for the rest of us, remember?"

"I love her."

All eyes on us now, the room is eerily silent. I take a hold of

Seph's hand, lacing our fingers together. No longer will we hide. No longer will we be afraid.

Seph steps closer to me, our arms brushing together now. "And I him. Regardless, we must stand up against injustice. I understand this is the Underworld. But there is still an order to things. It's up to us to make sure no one steps outside of their power, lest they take more than their share. He's done that. Not just with me, but with all of you, in some capacity."

We all know who she means when she says 'he.'

Hypnos whistles. "Well, I've never felt more awake. You two are finally an item, huh?"

"We have been for quite some time." Seph and I look at each other as she continues, "We didn't want anyone else to be hurt by knowing. I'm sorry we kept this from you all until now."

Megaera is the first to express her understanding, and others nod in agreement. No one objects.

Seph stares at the Mnemosyne River a few paces ahead of us. The dark cerulean water flows, slow and steady, carrying the memories lost to the Lethe. Her memories included. When she looks over her shoulder, eyes wide and brimming with tears, I run to her.

"We're all here, Seph. I'm here. It's okay."

Quiet enough for only me to hear, she asks, "What if this changes everything?"

"It most certainly will. But what will not change is that we are all here, and that I am here. My love for you will not change. Even if yours for me wavers, I'll be here in whatever capacity you desire. Do you understand?"

"It'll never waver. Will you go in with me?"

"I'll be right behind you. I swear to you, I won't let go."

After a few tentative steps, Seph's robe dampens and clings to her skin. As I follow her, my teeth chatter. I force my jaw shut as the cold water engulfs us. My arms wrap around her waist, and her hands find my biceps as she dunks her head under the water.

The minute that Seph stays underwater feels like an eon. I wait for her to emerge, beside myself but staying brave. I am not the one reliving multiple lifetimes's worth of horrors. She needs me here, holding her and strong.

Seph emerges with a sharp gasp for air. She slicks her soaked hair out of her eyes, then says the words none of us expect to hear.

"Hades killed Persephone." She says it like it happened to someone else, not her in a past life. Seph reaches for me, fisting my robe over my chest. I can feel her shiver in my arms, so I reposition her so I'm carrying her like she's my bride and walk her out of the water.

Hypnos is more awake than I've ever seen him. "Are you sure?"

"He's the one who stuck the dagger in her heart." Seph swallows. "In *my* heart, I suppose I should say. But I have a plan. I need to go to the Lethe."

CHAPTER 20

SEPH

As Thanatos leads me out of the Mnemosyne, Hynpos removes his fur-lined cloak and drapes it over me in Thanatos's arms as best as he can. "There. That should help you warm up."

I remember so much my body shakes.

The abduction. The bargain. The bloom of spring I was born to bring and the winters that came every time he forced me back underground. My rage, my loneliness, my desperate love for the mortal world. The taste of pomegranate seeds like sweet poison on my tongue. The ache of being torn in two with every changing season.

I remember every time Hades—and Zeus—touched me like I was something he owned.

Every time he whispered that I was helpless without him.

Every time I prayed to forget.

The Furies stand on the bank, eyes sharp and wary. Megaera's expression flickers between shock and something like pride. Alecto tilts her head, a slow smile curling her lips. Tisiphone hums tunelessly, eyes darting between us, restless and unblinking. My daughter, my sweet and tortured daughter, is still here too, waiting to see if I need her. Once Thanatos sets me down, I embrace her. She's given me so much, been through so much, that I cannot ever repay her.

Power hums in my veins like a storm ready to break. When I close my eyes, I see every moment of my imprisonment, every winter forced on a world that cried out for spring. I remember every seed, every lie, every stolen choice.

"I can take it from here."

"Are you sure?"

Thanatos says, "I'm going with you." As I split from my girl, I look back to him. The fear in his eyes doesn't diminish the fierce devotion I find there. His hand brushes my cheek, thumb tracing a wet lock of hair from my face. "I'll follow you to the end," he whispers.

My heart aches. My soul burns. I feel the ghosts of my past settle into my bones like armor.

I am more than just a lavender farmer.

The Lethe glitters in the dark like a black mirror, its slow, swirling waters reflecting the firelight around us. The river is silent—no babbling, no rush over stones—just an eerie, soundless current that winds like a snake through the roots of the Underworld. Mist hovers low, coiling around the banks, whispering to itself in voices I can almost hear. Voices of all the forgotten shades, I wager.

My sandals sink into the soft mud as I step closer. I grip the small crystal vial I brought in my pouch so tightly the cut-glass edges bite into my palm. The cork shakes in my other hand.

Each breath comes shallow and sharp. If we're caught here, it won't be a punishment. It'll be an execution.

Thanatos stands behind me, his presence a dark shield at my back. He hasn't said a word since we left the Mnemosyne, but he doesn't have to. I can feel both his anxiety and resolve rolling off him.

"Is it really this simple?" I whisper. My voice sounds small against the vast silence of the river. "A few drops of Lethe, and he'll forget?"

"Maybe not everything, but possibly," Thanatos says softly, his breath warm against my ear. "The river takes what it wants. But if you bind your intent to it, it will seek out the memories you name. You must have meant for it to swallow yours whole."

I swallow hard. The plan is as reckless as it is simple: spike the nectar Dionysus gifted me with the Lethe's water. Pour it for Hades at dinner. Let the river's magic erase his memory of me and of his unchallenged rule. When he wakes lost and confused, I'll have Thanatos reap him, and we'll banish him to Tartarus. Without him, the Underworld's throne will be mine by right—and with Thanatos at my side, we can build something better. Something fair.

Or we'll die trying, I suppose.

I sink to one knee at the river's edge, lifting the vial to the Lethe's surface. I watch the dark water swirl, and a sick shiver slides down my spine. To think I'd once lost everything here, to be drifted out to the Mnemosyne. My reflection ripples on its surface, and I remember how desperate I felt when he'd stabbed my chest. How hurt I'd been, not physically but mentally. How broken.

In my new life, I'd reforged myself. Now, I am adamant. I cannot break.

Thanatos' hand comes down on my shoulder, grounding

me. I feel the tremor in his fingers even through his gloves. "Careful," he murmurs. "Would hate to lose you again."

I bite my lip and lower the vial until the glass mouth kisses the water. The Lethe moves unnaturally, as if reaching up, eager to be taken. When I draw the vial back, clear liquid curls inside, looking no different than normal water. I cork it fast and clutch it to my chest. The moment it's sealed, a strange emptiness spreads across the bank, as if the river itself knows something has been stolen.

With unsteady legs, I stand. Thanatos's arm slips around my waist, supporting me. I lean into him, my forehead pressing to the cold, hard plane of his chest. For a few seconds, we just breathe, mist swirling around our feet.

"Are you sure?" he asks quietly. His voice is so raw it scrapes across my heart.

I lift my eyes to his, the vial trapped between us like a dark star. "This is the only way."

He searches my face as if trying to memorize every freckle, every line, every fear. His hand comes up to cradle my cheek. "If we fail..."

"I know," I say. My voice doesn't shake, even though everything else in me does. "If we fail, there will be nothing left of us."

I lean up and kiss him. Slow and deep, our mouths move together in a promise that tastes like fire and brimstone. When we break apart, he rests his forehead against mine.

"Then we can't fail," he whispers.

The walk back is the longest of my life.

Every shadow seems alive. Every gust of cold air carries whispers of Hades's voice, and it makes me more paranoid than usual. Thanatos keeps me close, his stride long and silent, the folds of his robe swallowing any light. We slip through Elysium's sleeping woods, across the dark banks of the Styx, and back into the warren of tunnels beneath the Palace that I hadn't even known were there. By the time we reach my chambers, my heart feels like it's going to tear itself apart.

Inside, the warmth of my hearth feels almost obscene. I extinguish it as fast as I can, wanting nothing more to do with the heat. Underfoot, my thick rugs muffle our steps, and my vanity glitters with trinkets and jewelry from my past life that only now I recognize. I set the vial of Lethe carefully down, next to the bottle of Dionysus's nectar. Its glass glows faintly, infused with the god's wild, drunken magic.

With my son's wild, drunken magic. The thought of what they did to my boy is enough to make me weep, but I hold it all in. Now is not the time to dwell on past hurt. Now is the time to act on them.

Thanatos eyes it with a mix of awe and dread. "Once you add it, there's no going back."

"I know," I whisper. I uncork the nectar bottle and slip the Lethe vial's stopper free. The river water gleams as it spills drop by drop into the deep, amber liquid. Each drop curls in the nectar like a serpent before disappearing, swallowed whole. At a glance, no one would ever know. When I sniff it, too, it smells the same. I cork the bottle with shaking hands.

Thanatos stands behind me, his hands resting on my shoulders. His grip is cool, yet heavy with the weight of everything unspoken. I close my eyes, leaning back into him, letting his breath ruffle my hair.

"You're sure he'll drink it?" I ask.

"He's never turned down one of Dionysus's gifts. While he

wants nothing to do with the rest of the Olympians, he knows that was one his son. So he tries to play nice with Dionysus, at least."

A muscle jumps in his jaw. I know Thanatos hates this. Hates letting me anywhere near Hades. But he knows, as I do, that it has to be me. Hades will never suspect I'm capable of such treachery. He still thinks I'm meek. Broken. His perfect little pomegranate.

Thanatos' arms slip around me fully, pulling me tight against him. His lips brush the crown of my head. "Seph, if anything happens—"

"It won't," I cut in, fierce. For my own sanity, to convince myself this will work, I *have* to be fierce. I turn in his arms, cupping his face between my hands. "This ends now. I'm done living as his shadow. Done letting him decide who I am."

The shadows outside my window ripple, the palace groaning low in its foundation. It feels like the Underworld itself is listening, holding its breath to see who shall rule it in the coming days. Thanatos kisses me, hard and desperate, and I feel his fear in every trembling inch of him.

When he pulls back, his eyes blaze. "Then let's finish this."

We speak quickly, laying the plan out again in hushed voices to make sure we haven't missed any gaps. For a moment, we stare at each other. I see the terror and the hope in his eyes, the things he'll never say because there's no time left.

I squeeze his fingers. "When the bottle is empty," I whisper, "be ready. I'll rub my pendant."

"When will you do it?"

"Next time he tries to woo me, I suppose. He insinuated before that his patience will only go so far. I never thought I'd say this, but now I hope he does pursue me so we can get this over with."

I can never—will never—let him steal another spring.

CHAPTER 21

THANATOS

Another war on the surface means another influx of shades. Hades drowns in paperwork, and I'm running to and from the surface more than ever. Tragedy never stops on the surface anymore, and when I asked Seph for a mortal's perspective, she shrugged and said she wished she had the answer. That men on the surface, too, crave power just as much as the gods do. I know she's right, since Ares tends to the perpetrators and I tend to the innocents. The women, the children, men caught in the wrong place at the wrong time or with the wrong skin color.

Maybe that's why she's so calm in the days leading up to her plan; she's used to this by now. Survival mode is nothing new for her. We don't have a set date, and she's trying to make herself more available for Hades. But with the newest batch to process, Hades doesn't have time for her.

So we wait.

When I finally have a night off after what feels like an eon, I beeline it for her chambers. I need to feel her in my arms, need to cherish her. After so much death and destruction, my own soul feels weary.

From her bed, I spread my legs wide, sitting up against the pillows and headboard. When I pat the space between my thighs, Seph joins me, tucking her knees up as she leans her back against my chest. Ever since her dip in the river, her memories have been plaguing her day and night. I can tell from the darkness now in her eyes, and Hypnos tipped me off about her dreams as of late. When I'm unable to tend to her or comfort her, my brother sneaks into her dreams to make them more pleasant.

After everything she's been through, it's a wonder she's still sane. Still standing.

I place one hand on her hip, and she immediately reaches for it to interlace our fingers. When I drape my other hand across the top of her chest, she repeats the motion, keeping us woven together as I embrace her. My heart breaks as she trembles in my arms, so I press kisses to her neck, softer than usual. I'm so used to killing whoever I touch that I'm still scared to hold her sometimes, still kiss her like she's made of porcelain and not a goddess reborn. I suppose love will do that to a man.

Seph tilts her head back, granting me more access to the column of her throat. I kiss her more, slow and steady. Grounding. I'm here, in my own quiet way. I've got her, and I'm never letting her go.

Not even as Hades opens the door.

Seph whirls to look at him, and I face a choice. I can teleport us away, even though we've already been caught. Or, I can own up to this. Leaving her alone with him isn't an option.

I pull her closer to my chest. Her hands squeeze mine as she looks back at me.

"It's okay. I'm here," I whisper. "It's okay."

Because after how much he has tortured her, I want nothing more than to kill Hades where he stands. The rage bubbles in my chest, so strong I could grab it with my hands and mold it into a weapon of my design. But I hold it back, channeling it into protecting the innocent woman in my arms.

I remember she has stained her hands with blood. For a good cause, yes, but not as innocent as the maid of spring she used to be. Hades may have intended for Seph's mortal life to be a cage, but it will be the thing to set her free.

Hades scoffs when he sees us. "Drop the doe-eyed act, Persephone. Don't think I haven't known."

"How long have you suspected?"

"Since I first saw Thanatos enter that damned garden of yours." He looks at me, scorn in his fiery gaze. "You are a traitor. I'd kill you now, were it not for her being in your arms."

He won't hurt her. This is good. Seph realizes how much Hades has revealed too, because she squeezes my hands.

Hades spits on the ground, and his saliva is so hot it sizzles when it hits the stone. "Out of all the fools in this damned place, of all the fucking gods, I never thought you might be the one to betray me, Thanatos. Never thought you'd be the one to dare slither between my wife's legs."

"I'm not your wife," Seph barks back. "I may have been once. In the mortal realm, we have a saying when couples wed: til death do us part. Death parted us when Persephone was murdered in the river that day."

Hades bristles at her statement, at her bold defiance. "Know your place, *kore*." There's venom in his voice when he calls her *kore*.

"You've no right to call me that. And I do know my place. Wife I may not be anymore, my soul is still my soul. That makes me a ruler of this hellhole. My power lingers, right there with your loneliness." She scowls at him, a look I've never seen on her face. "You're no better than the men of the mortal realm."

"How dare you!"

"It's true. They take what they want, rape us rather than

woo us because they feel they are owed for no reason other than having a worm between their legs. You'd rather pluck a maiden from the fields or kill her before her time than actually care for her, respect her like she deserves. Like *I* deserve. Well newsflash. God or not, your loneliness is not my responsibility, nor is it my job to fix. You are owed nothing."

Hades surges forward, but I untangle one of our hands to summon my scythe. I hold the blade by his bearded chin, and it's enough to give Hades pause. I don't flex my power often, but I know Seph won't run. Won't be afraid.

What happens next surprises me and Hades alike.

Seph lets go of my hands and grabs my scythe, holding the blade directly up to Hades' throat. She stands and presses it enough to shave his beard, black hairs falling to the stone floor. "If you hurt a single hair on his head," Seph says as Hades' eyes widen, "then not even Zeus will be able to contain my wrath. Do you understand? The Persephone you once knew is gone. You beat her for so long, and she saw too much in her mortal life to not walk away unchanged. And guess what, Hades? Beaten dogs bite back, and I've every intention to be the bitch of your worst nightmares."

"Give the scythe back to Thanatos. You don't know what you're doing."

"Don't I?" She smirks, and I wonder if that expression was the last thing the man she killed saw. The man who hurt her friend the way Hades has hurt her. "I was reborn a lavender farmer. How do you think we harvest the fields? How do you think I killed a man for committing the same sins as you?"

"A compromise, then. Thanatos and I shall fight for your hand. To the death." Hades looks at me, eyes narrowing. If I don't agree, my reputation as a reaper is ruined. If I agree and lose, it's ruined anyway.

I've no choice but to go down swinging. And for Seph, I will.

"I'll do it."

"We fight in the training pits in three nights."

I swallow thickly. "You can lower the scythe now, Seph."

She doesn't. Instead, she looks Hades in his garnet eyes and says, "I will never be yours."

"We'll see about that."

She presses the scythe further. Why he doesn't fight back when he'd been so ready to move at her initial defiance is beyond me. My scythe must make all the difference, a note I make for our upcoming duel.

"One last thing." Seph's eyes darken, the fire of the Underworld fueling her. "You should ask Zeus about my children. Melinoë and Zagreus."

Her word choice strikes me instantly. Not their children—*her* children.

Hades all but growls. "What are you implying?"

"You know your brother and his reputation well enough to know the answer to that question."

Seph lowers the scythe, handing it to me without turning her back on Hades. Her eyes don't leave him as she steps back, making just enough room for him to leave her chambers.

The silence is loud as the realization dawns on him, contorting his features. It explains everything: why Melinoë is so tortured by the madness and nightmares she reigns over, why Hera grew jealous over Zagreus's existence enough to have the boy torn limb from limb. Hades goes through all seven stages of grief at once and leaves without further comment.

No matter who wins the duel, Seph has made one thing clear: she will be the victor no matter what happens.

CHAPTER 22

SEPH

U nsure of what the next three days may bring, we spend all of our time before the duel together. I refuse to say or admit that this could be my last time with Thanatos, but deep within my soul, I know the risks. Hades is strong, and the shades all fear him for good reason.

We train, ensuring Thanatos is strong enough. Then, our last night comes faster than I'd like.

We're alone in my garden, the trees full and heavy with pomegranates. Sharing one, we relish in the taste, the fruits of our labor, the seeds inside the outer shell. I'm so nervous, though, I can barely stand to eat, so I end up feeding the seeds to Thanatos instead. I don't think he's craving food, either, but he wraps his lips around each with care and eats them anyway. Both of our fingertips and lips are stained magenta with the juice by the time we finish.

Thanatos is the one to break our silence. He looks me in the eyes, looking not like the God of Death but like a scared man in love.

"Know this, little butterfly. No matter what happens, even if

I die tomorrow, it will be worth it. It'll be worth it because I got to know you, to have you, to love you."

My throat feels like it's going to close as pressure builds behind my eyes. I can't cry, not now. I need to be confident for the both of us. "You're going to win, Than. You have to."

"I'm going to try. But I can't make that promise. For once, I'm evenly matched."

"I'll stop it before things get to that point. I won't let you die."

"If I do, it's okay, Seph. I'd rather love you for a brief time than not love you at all."

"Please don't talk like this. Like you won't win."

"I understand now, what the mortals fear. Why they panic. They fight for this."

I brush his hair back, wanting to linger on his face. To memorize every colored fleck in his eyes while I still can. "I love you. We've an immortal lifetime ahead of us."

Then his mouth is everywhere: at my throat, my collarbone, my lips. Each kiss feels like it brands me, staking a claim deeper than words ever could. My body arches into his, desperate, aching, greedy for every brush of his hands.

He murmurs my name like a prayer. It's raw and hungry and so tender it nearly undoes me. When he moves inside me, slow at first, like he's afraid I'll break, a soft cry escapes my lips. I've never known a touch like his, careful and feral all at once, where every thrust is a promise and a plea. If he fails, I'll live in solitude. None can compare to Thanatos, to this.

I don't want to think about the danger. About who might be watching through the shadows right now on what very well may be our final night together. About the price waiting for us at the end of this road. But I can't stop the thought from slipping through the comforting chill of his kiss: if Hades wins, it's all over.

The fear coils around the edges of my mind, but Thanatos's hands soothe it back. He whispers things I can barely hear over the rush of blood in my ears. Sweet, desperate words make my chest ache and legs tremble. I press my mouth to his neck, tasting the salt from our sweat and the leftover pomegranate on my tongue. Thanatos gasps when I roll my hips, and the sound shreds the last of my fear. I want more. I want *everything*. To hear him come apart, to watch the God of Death fall to his knees for me and never stand again.

Because in this moment, my fear leaves me. I'm not scared of Hades, not of the Fates, not of death itself. In this moment, there is only the two of us, our bodies tangled in my bedsheets, my phantom heart thundering like a war drum, our souls reaching across the void for something neither of us has ever dared believe we could have: each other.

When release finally comes, it rips through me like a wave. Every nerve in my body is alight, every cry swallowed by his lips. I cling to him as we fall together, the world shrinking to the ragged rise and fall of my chest and the soft, broken sounds we make in each other's arms.

As he kisses me, I feel the weight of the nectar bottle in my pouch at my hip. I know this: I will burn this realm to the ground before I let Hades take him from me.

Thanatos stays in my bed, though we don't make love a second time. I want him energized, not exhausted from a day full of trysts. With a final kiss in the morning, he bids me farewell, and I bid him luck.

I bring the nectar with me and head to the training rooms.

Part of me mourns the space; I once associated it with days training with the Furies, days that accounted to nothing because it all comes down to this. Of course, Hades wouldn't want to touch a hair on my head. Not until he's won me as his prize, anyway. I must remain unsoiled until then.

Melinoë rushes beside me in the stands, where I sit with the Furies and Hypnos.

"Bad news," Melinoë says in a hushed whisper. "The dagger. It's been stolen."

"Not stolen," Alecto says, gesturing to the pit. "Retrieved. Look."

Torchlight flickers wildly across the dirt floor, the flames turning sickly green every time Hades shifts his weight. The god lounges in the center of the pit, his armor a deep crimson shot through with black veins. He watches Thanatos with a heavy, disdainful calm, eyes glowing like coals. The adamant dagger—the same one I remember sinking into my chest in—hangs loosely from his hand, its blade drinking in the torchlight.

Fucking bastard.

When he stands, he towers over Thanatos, who isn't short by any means. Thanatos's scythe glints like a sliver of midnight in his white-knuckled grip. Shadows gather around him, drawn to his anger like iron to a lodestone.

For a heartbeat, no one moves. The whole palace holds its breath.

Hades's lips curve into a slow, mocking smile. "You dare to raise your blade to me, little reaper?" His voice rumbles through the stone floor beneath the dirty, deep and resonant, like the earth itself is cracking open. He lifts the dagger, twirling it easily between his fingers. "I didn't think you'd actually show up. Do you think your pitiful love grants you power over death itself?"

Thanatos doesn't flinch. His voice is low, every word cutting and deliberate. "Know your place. I do not fear death," he says. His silver eyes catch the light, hard and unyielding. "I *am* death."

Hades' laugh is a low, cruel thing, rolling across the hall. "Then prove it."

The words hang for the barest moment. Then everything explodes.

Thanatos lunges first, scythe arcing in a blur of black steel. Hades meets him with a vicious downward slash of his dagger. The clash of adamant rings like a cracked bell, echoes bouncing between the pillars. Sparks flare at their feet, casting wild shadows up the walls.

I stagger back, the thunderous force of their first collision rattling the floor beneath me. My heart seizes in my chest as the two gods whirl together, blades flashing faster than thought. Thanatos is a phantom, cloak swirling, feet dancing over shattered marble as he presses the attack. He's at full power, and it's nothing short of impressive. If I didn't know him like I do, I'd be terrified.

But Hades moves like an avalanche: unstoppable, crushing, every blow of his dagger aimed to maim or kill. His eyes burn with a cruel light that pins me in place, as if even mid-battle, he never forgets that this is all for me.

They break apart, circling each other. Black mist coils from Thanatos' scythe with every breath he takes, shadows reaching for Hades like hungry hands. The god of the dead only laughs, the sound echoing up to the vaulted ceiling.

"You think you can take her from me?" Hades bellows, voice thick with rage. His dagger gleams like a shard of frozen night as he lunges. "You think you are worthy of my queen?"

Thanatos parries hard, their blades locking. His snarl tears through the air. "She was never yours."

The words hit me like lightning.

Their weapons clash again and again, each impact a shock-wave of noise. Thanatos slips under a savage slash, scythe carving a deadly arc, but Hades spins away, dagger hissing past Thanatos' ribs. A thin line of blood blooms on his tunic, stark against black.

Thanatos would rather die than see me chained again. What happens to Death if he, himself dies? That can't happen. I reach for my pouch hanging from my waistbelt, feeling the nectar inside.

Hades's grin is a crescent moon of malice. "She chose me once," he sneers. "She will again."

"No," Thanatos growls. His voice is thunder. His scythe blurs, and I see death itself in every sweep of his blade. "You stole her choice. Never again."

They clash together in a storm of metal and fury, the training grounds shaking beneath the weight of their power. In the stands, I stand frozen—terrified, furious, desperate—because I know only one of them will walk away.

And it has to be him. It *has* to be.

I nearly blink and miss it. Hades lunges, but gets cocky, and leaves an opening. Thanatos takes it, scythe slashing across the gap, and the blade makes contact.

He cleaves Hades' head off. The god's skull thuds against the dirt, puffing up sand. But there is no time to celebrate, to claim victory, because a mere second later, his head grows back.

With new skin, Hades laughs. "Did you really think it would be so easy to kill me?"

CHAPTER 23
THANATOS

Panic creeps in, but I push it back. There's no time to panic. Panic will make me sloppy. There is no wiggle room for that.

I take a deep breath, steeling myself for the fight ahead. While Hades shows no sign of slowing down, I don't either. As two death gods, this fight could last days. Weeks. Maybe even years.

Hades holds his head high, beard reaching its full length from before Seph chopped it three nights ago. He licks the small strip of my blood off the adamant blade and says, "A shame. You were once my best soldier, Thanatos. Now, I have to kill you with the same blade I used to kill her. Poetic, don't you think?"

I don't give him the satisfaction of a response. He wants to throw me off, to use psychological warfare in this battle of arms. Hoping my comrade-in-arms Ares guides me, I ready my scythe once more. My muscles burn with each swing, each block, each parry. I try to create distance, using the length of the handle to my advantage. But with Hades's dagger, he takes every chance he gets to close the distance. What I lack in size compared to him, though, I make up for with agility.

Sweat drips into my eyes as blood runs down my side. My arms shake from the force of our blows. But the thought of Seph taken, terrified, and chained back to his throne drives every scrap of strength I have left into my limbs.

I whirl my scythe once more, and as Hades meets it with his dagger, sparks explode. Our blades lock, faces inches apart. His eyes gleam with ancient madness, a man so lonely it's driven him to greed rather than empathy.

"For every seed you forced down her throat," I say, pressing my weight into the clash, "I will rip you apart again and again, until you stay dead."

His smile is a crescent of blood and shadow. "You're slowing down, little reaper."

He feints left, then drives the adamant dagger straight for my heart. I twist just in time. The blade carves a burning line across my ribs, hot blood soaking into my tunic. The pain flashes white behind my eyes, staggering me. My scythe dips, the tip gouging a furrow into the dirt.

Hades's laugh scrapes over my raw nerves. "Did you truly believe you could best me in my own realm?" He stalks forward, every step unhurried, certain. "You are nothing. A child of night, born to ferry souls, not to challenge a king."

I raise my scythe, but the weight feels unbearable now. His decapitation didn't just give him a new head, but a burst of stamina. My vision tunnels on the gleam of his dagger.

"No!" Seph's voice pierces the din, wild and furious. But it sounds so far away.

Hades lunges. I barely bring my scythe up in time to block, and the force drives me to one knee. His shadow looms over me, dagger high. The world narrows to the point of his blade, descending straight for my throat.

I'm going to fail her, I think, panic choking me. *I'm going to lose.*

But before the dagger can strike, from the stands, I hear the voice I'd recognize anywhere: "Stop!"

We both turn to see Seph, tears flowing down her face on the sidelines. My instinct is to run to her, to embrace her, but with this monster above me, I am stuck in place.

"Please, both of you, stop."

As she runs into the ring, I notice the pouch hanging from her belt. Her taking action causes Hades to step away from me and toward her, large hand outstretched.

"Persephone, back away. It's not safe for you here. This traitor has poisoned your mind with lies and falsehoods. Let me handle this."

"I don't want this." Tears stream down her cheeks, and she's openly weeping as she speaks. "Please, Hades, listen to me. Promise you'll hear me out."

"I promise."

"If you promise not to hurt Thanatos, to walk away from this fight, I won't lie with him again. I never shall, so long as we're here together."

No. *No.* I go to speak up, but in my peripheral, I catch Melinoë. She holds her finger to her lips, shushing me. I heed her advice and let Seph do what she must.

Hades, for whatever it's worth, listens to her. I'd been fully prepared to lay my life on the line so Seph could have her freedom, but it appears that won't be necessary. I just hope she knows what she's doing.

Hades says her name, but is otherwise too stunned to say anything else.

Seph reaches into her pouch, procuring a glass bottle of golden liquid. *The nectar.* She never got to give it to him. "Here. We've gotten off on the wrong foot. I've made mistakes, but I remember everything now. So to apologize, and to start over, I wanted to offer you this. Nectar, as a peace and love offering. I got it from Dionysus to give to you."

I've never seen the Lord of the Underworld so stunned. There's hope in his eyes, real and tangible and undeniable. Some part of him truly loved her, I think, in his own fucked up way. Or, at the very least, he loved controlling her, having one of the most beautiful people in Olympus to call his own.

In a sense, Hades and I are alike. He never took another lover after Persephone's death. He never took one before her, either. We both deal in death, feared for it and isolated as a result. But I do not feel I am owed her. I am not owed anything from anyone. Hades, however, felt entitled to her. Not once, but twice.

And now, he's about to pay for it. My little butterfly will defeat the Lord of the Underworld not with brute strength, but with her smarts.

Hades takes the nectar. "Do you remember now? Truly? Are you back to me?"

"I remember everything, Hades. I went to the Mnemosyne. Everything."

"So my wife returns at last. The Queen of the Underworld is finally home."

"I am."

"Then you'll drink with me, yes?" He holds out the nectar bottle to her, and I feel bile rise to my throat. *No no no no.* She can't drink it. Has he seen right through her? Is he calling her bluff? I hold my breath, not wanting to move a muscle, not wanting to do anything that might betray her ruse.

"Of course. But you first. You're still Master of the Palace, after all. And besides, I'd be a terrible gift-giver if I took the first swig."

Hades chuckles, amused by her words. By the gods, she's done it. She's tricked him. He believes her, so overcome with joy at the thought that he won and got what he wanted after all that he's not thinking clearly.

It's the only explanation for why he uncorks it then drinks. The bottle is dwarfed in his hands, and he chugs half of it without trying.

And it's enough to send Hades stepping back. The bottle tumbles to the ground, shattering against the tile and sending nectar across Hades's feet. No one says his name. No one except for Seph moves as Hades stares at his hands, then at her.

"Wh... wh... wh..." He repeats the sound for a few minutes, babbling like a toddler learning to speak. Eventually, he finds the words. "Who am I?"

Leaning against my scythe, I stand as Seph answers, "You're a shade."

"A shade?"

"A soul. A spirit." Vines grow beneath the dirt, stemming from her feet and crawling up Hades's legs. Even from where I am, I can see the thorns lining them, sharp enough to pierce Hades's armor. "Damned to this place with the rest of us."

"Who are you?"

Seph smirks. "The Queen of the Underworld. All here bow to my reign."

To emphasize her point, I bow. Melinoë, my brother, and the Fury sisters all take a knee, lowering their heads. She holds her hand out to me, an invitation. As I bring her knuckles to my lips, she says, "Reap him."

As I drop her hand, I grip my scythe. "As Her Majesty wishes."

My strength returns with every breath. Time seems to slow. I step forward, my footsteps not so much as echoing. Hades's gaze locks onto me, dark eyes wide. and for the first time, I see it: fear. The same fear every soul knows at the end.

I raise my scythe high, shadows rising around me like a

cloak. The air grows heavy with the scent of earth after rain, the hush before the final heartbeat. My scythe hums with the power of every life I've ever claimed, every soul I've ever ferried beyond the veil and brought to Hermes and Charon.

Hades opens his mouth to speak, but before he can, I bring the blade down.

The scythe slices through his chest like a stroke of midnight, light bursting in a silent explosion of silver and green. His scream never fully forms, the sound torn away as his soul is wrenched from his body in a shimmering storm of black and red. Shadows scatter like frightened birds. The air ripples with raw, ancient power, then stills. His body dissipates, leaving his spectral form behind.

Seph turns to the River Styx, and the moment she calls for Charon, his boat is there. He stands tall and impossibly thin, his dark robes drifting around him like a tattered shroud caught in a current. His skeletal face peers out from beneath the shadow of his hood, features bleached white as moonlit bone. Twin pinpricks of blue light burn in the sockets where his eyes should be, shifting to me, then to Seph. His presence carries the cold, wet scent of river water and old coins.

Behind him floats his vessel of blackened wood that looks older than the Underworld itself. Its hull is slick with algae, carved with runes so worn they've nearly vanished. The prow curves like a serpent's neck, ending in a grinning skull.

His voice is more of a rasp. "Yes, Your Majesty?"

"Escort this lost soul away, please. It looks like he doesn't have any memories. May he ponder on this in solitude until we hold court next and I decide where he belongs." From her pouch, she retrieves an obol, flicking it to Charon. The ferryman catches it with a bony hand. As Hades is whisked away, he takes in his surroundings like he's seeing everything for the first time. He might as well be.

Justice has been served.

The vessel glides away into the mist, fading as quickly as it arrived, the faint chime of Charon's coins the only sign he was ever there. Once Charon is so far down the River Styx they're out of sight, Seph sighs in relief.

Alecto, with a wicked and wild grin, says, "All Hail the Queen of the Underworld."

But Seph pays her no mind as she whirls to me, immediately assessing me. "Than? Are you okay? He didn't hurt you, did he?"

I wince as her fingertips graze the cut across my ribs. "I'm fine, Seph. Nothing that won't heal by morning."

She looks me up and down thrice over anyway, only stopping when I take her hands in mine.

"Seph. You did it."

The Underworld is free of Hades at last. For the first time, the palace feels truly silent—not the silence of fear or oppression, but of peace settling over these ancient, hallowed halls.

CHAPTER 24
SEPH

I approach the throne of bones in the great hall. To think I once feared this seat, the man who sat in it. Behind me, Thanatos sneaks up. His voice catches my attention, given his footsteps are as silent as ever.

"It's strange to see it without anyone on it."

I look at him from over my shoulder before turning to face him. "Is it? It's just a chair."

"To you, sure. But to the shades here, it's a symbol of power. And now, it's yours for the taking."

I smile at him as I sit, feeling the smooth texture beneath me. The years haven't been kind to these bones. I can't help but wonder whose they were, from whence they came. Thousands of years of history, all smelted into this chair. This throne.

Thanatos has a point. Whether I respected it or not, this seat holds power. As does whoever claimed it.

"Better?" I ask as I sit.

Thanatos chuckles, the way he does near-silently from his chest. "Oh, I much prefer this. A welcome change." He strides closer, hands clasped behind his back, looking ever the dutiful subject. Except he isn't a subject, not to me.

No, none of this would be possible without Thanatos.

I ask, "Have you ever sat in it?"

"Never."

"Would you like to?"

"It's not my place."

"Isn't it?" I rise and stand to the side, right in front of one the arms.

Thanatos bows his head, a light smile playing at his lips. If he could blush, I think he would be right now. "My Lady, I'd never be so presumptuous."

"You're my equal, Than. I'm inviting you."

Thanatos takes the last few steps up the dais, then—without taking his eyes off mine—sits upon the throne. His leg spread, and the dark robe he wears shifts, revealing his skin—so pale it's almost gray—and taught thigh muscles.

"And where, My Lady, will you sit if I'm using your throne?"

I run my hand along the top of the bones, noticing the sheer size of the throne. It's massive; Thanatos could be twice the size he is and still fit in it. So I lift the skirts of my robe and straddle his waist, my feet hooking over the tops of his thighs. Thanatos's hands go to my hips, like it's his instinct to reach out for me.

"Right here, of course."

He raises a brow at me. "In such a public display?"

He's teasing, I can tell, so I match his tone. "Are you questioning your queen?"

"Why, I wouldn't dare." He captures my mouth with his then, hands running from my ribs to my spine. It's not long before his tongue moves past my lips. In case there are any questions about my intentions, I grind my hips against his. Only the fabric of his robe separates us, and I can feel him hardening beneath me. His hips meet mine, but he doesn't shift his chiton yet.

After a few moments of this, Thanatos tugs his robe to the side. Before I can ride him, though, he pulls his lips away. "Stand. Turn around."

Curious as to where he's going with this, I obey. As soon as my back is to him, Thanatos unclasps my robe's fastener. It falls to my ankles, then once I step out of it, he pulls me back onto his lap. I adjust my legs so I can straddle him once more, completely bare as I face the throne room.

Thanatos's hands wrap around my body, reaching up until he cups my breasts. I sink onto him, earning a loud groan that echoes through the room.

"I want even Tartarus to hear us," I tell him. "I don't want us to have to hide anymore."

"We don't have to hide. All this, this entire domain," Thanatos presses his lips to my neck, "is yours. As am I."

His thumbs rub circles over my nipples as his teeth sink into my shoulder, not hard enough to pierce skin but enough to imprint. The slight edge of pain only amplifies the pleasure. Thanatos releases his teeth and leans back to give me more room, and my back arches as I ride his cock until he's fully sheathed in me.

As I rock my hips, I feel his piercing hitting the perfect spot within me. That combined with the fullness of him, all while we share this throne, shoots waves of pleasure through my body. Life and Death, united at last with no one to stop us.

In my ear, Thanatos whispers, "Imagine holding court like this? With you, doing your duty as queen from atop my cock? And me, ever your dutiful lover, ensuring you find pleasure while the whole Underworld watches? Only filling you with my cum when you tell me to?"

"You want me to edge you on, Thanatos?"

"Of course I do. For I am Death Incarnate, and you are Life. I cannot exist without you, cannot function without you, so I submit fully to you. My butterfly, I am at your will and mercy in all things. Including this."

His words are enough to have me clenching on him, and I hear him hum in acknowledgement—or maybe its appreciation, or both—against my shoulder. Then he shudders hard, forehead pressed to my shoulder, his groan so deep it vibrates through my body. His grip on me turns bruising as he rides out his orgasm, hips stuttering, breath uneven.

For a long, suspended moment, we sit there, a queen and her loyal soldier. I can taste tears on my lips, the laughter that wants to bubble up because we're alive, we're together, and we've done the unthinkable. For this stolen heartbeat, we are gods of our own making—unbowed, unbroken, and more dangerous together than we could ever be apart.

Slowly, the world filters back in: the hiss of the torches guttering low along the walls, the scent of spent candles and cold marble, everything that now lays before us. With Hades dead, I have large shoes to fill. A lot needs changing.

As we clean up and adjust our robes, Thanatos asks, "So what's your first order as the sole ruler, Your Majesty?"

"I want to free all of this women. Send them to Elysium. But before we get into that, I'd like to do one thing. Visit one place. Can you take me there?"

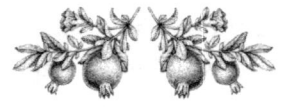

As the personification of Death, Thanatos can traverse the realms. We have Hypnos call Hermes for help so I can get there and back in one piece too, and I can't help but notice the way the two gods eye both Melinoë *and* one another. But with Hermes's blessing, we both make it to the surface in no time.

It's a relief to see home again. Not my apartment in the city that I moved to after college, but where I grew up. Lavender spreads across the fields, blooming bright and purple. Spring is in full bloom, the flowers ready for harvest. In the distance, the Olympic mountain range spreads across the horizon, still speckled with snow at the peaks. I feel both out of place, given my ancient Grecian attire, but also like I fit right in. Like the lavender responds to my touch, like I can control the sway of the stems.

In the fields, scythes in hand, I see my parents. They both look up after a few minutes of harvesting, and when they see me, they drop their farm tools.

"Persephone?"

All it takes for them to sprint to me is for me to wave. They embrace me in a tight hug, each of them burying their face in one of my shoulders.

Exasperated, my mother asks, "Where have you been? And what are you wearing?"

"It's a long story. I can't stay. But know that I'm safe and well."

"You haven't answered your phone in a year!"

"Has it been that long?" Maybe time moves differently down there. It feels like it's simultaneously been a month and a decade.

"Who's this man with you?"

I untangle from them and look back to see Thanatos with wide eyes. "They can see me?"

"Of course we can see you!" My father charges, fists balling. "Who the hell are you? Are you the one responsible for my daughter going missing?"

"Dad." I grip his shoulder. "It's not his fault. This is Thanatos."

My mother steps forward to join us. "Thanatos, huh? Another one named after a Greek god?"

Ignoring her, my father doesn't relent. "You disappear for a year, don't answer your phone. We sent out search and rescue parties, put out missing posters, everything. And nothing. No sign of you. It's like you vanished. Your friends said you were supposed to meet at a coffee shop, but when they got there, your table just had a cup of tea and a book on it. Then you show up dressed like you walked out of a costume shop with a strange man and you mean to tell me he's not responsible?"

Thanatos's eyes narrow. "I am the one who took your daughter, but on Hades's orders. I am not named after the Greek god. I am Death himself. Your daughter bears the same soul as Persephone, the goddess of spring, Queen of the Underworld. Were you not her mortal family, I'd make you fall to your knees to address my queen with more respect. But as I don't wish to upset my beloved, I will let your comments slide."

"Than, play nice."

"Are you on drugs?" My father scoffs. "Can you believe this, honey?"

"Dad, it's true," I say. "But I came to say goodbye. I won't be back."

My mother is the one who understands. "You took over for Hades, didn't you?" She gestures to Thanatos. "He called you his beloved."

"I did. I have an Underworld to rule. But I'll still be in contact with Demeter so the harvests aren't so terrible. I know the last few decades have been hard on the farm."

"We did always seem to get by a little better than the others," my mother recalls.

"One day," Thanatos says, "I will come for you. When it is your time, you shall have a place in our palace, should she deem it so."

My father leers. "Is that a threat?"

"No. It's a promise. Death comes for all mortals."

"Be nice to him," I warn my father. "He saved my soul. We'll meet again. Don't worry about me. I love you both."

As I grab Thanatos's hand, I take one last look at the lavender fields, the mountains, the sky. Then we vanish into the shadows, returning to the Underworld that has become my new home. When I return, free of Hades and hand-in-hand with Thanatos, it finally feels like one.

EPILOGUE

THANATOS

T he throne of bones is cool beneath my body. I lean back against the glorified chair, the bones feeling sturdy and smooth against my back and thighs. My legs spread enough for Seph to sit atop me comfortably, but with room for what she is about to do.

Seph wears a robe of all black, the cut of her neckline low enough to reveal ample cleavage. Her skin all but glows, radiant even in darkness. She smirks at me as she steps up on the dais, looking every bit of the queen she's become. Jewels drip down her body over her exposed slits of skin, adorning her chest and arms. A matching crown, freshly carved from obsidian, rests atop her head.

My cock, hard beneath my chiton, throbs. It springs out from the short fabric, slit in just the right spot to reveal to her as I sit this way. No one is in this chamber yet, but damned shades seeking an audience will be soon enough. We don't intend on stopping any time soon, either.

Seph smiles at me, sweet as a summer berry, as I shift the fabric of her robes. Once my hands graze the bare skin of her thighs, I trail my thumb up to her pussy. Running my finger from her clit down the center, I grin when I find her already wet and wanting.

"The anticipation alone is riling you up, isn't it?"

Through a breathy sigh, Seph says, "I see I'm not alone in that."

Still teasing her folds, I chuckle once. "Guilty as charged."

Seph hikes her robes up to her waist, turns, and lowers herself onto my cock. I groan in delight, hands immediately gripping her hips. Her robe drapes over the front of her, concealing—albeit barely—how she takes my cock. Whenever I drive up into her, her robe shifts just enough for the torchlight to filter in. In those moments, we are fully visible.

We spare our immediate relatives from the sight, relieving them of their duties for the day, but otherwise call court in session. Seph and I are aware of the eyes on us as I shift my hips ever so subtly, moving in and out of her at a languid pace. We're not obvious, but not discreet, either. Like its casual, normal—a flex of power in its own right.

Seph pardons some wrongfully judged souls, many whose stories I remember from their reaping. Seeing her fully realized in her power, even if we still have a long road ahead of us, only makes my cock harder. With her wet heat enveloping me, I'm not sure how much longer I can last, but like we fantasized, I'll hold on. Waiting for her command, so no one can mistake who is in charge here. I've no desire for ultimate power, trusting it within Seph's hands, but have no problem allowing people to fear my presence. I aim to please her, and should anyone object, I take no issue in sending them to their doom. My lover is the beginning, and I am the inevitable end.

As she clenches around me, I brush her hair over one shoulder. My lips reach the now exposed pane of her neck, and I press soft yet firm kisses there. Once, I wanted to shield her from the

Underworld. But Seph's done a wonderful job at making my home her own as well.

When she comes a second time a few shades later, hard enough that I feel her arousal dripping down me, she stops mid-sentence. The shades look at her expectantly, eyes wide at the sight of my beautiful love, their queen, riding the wave of pleasure.

Through her moan, she bids me to come with her.

So I join her, letting her squeeze around my cock until it's spent. I press an open-mouthed kiss to her neck, soaking up her warmth as I slow into a still. My dick twitches as my release continues, spilling outside her and joining her slick that drips on my balls.

She doesn't lift herself off me. Instead, she stays put, keeping me sheathed within her, skirt hiked up just enough for shades to catch a glimpse of our mess. In the past, I never would have guessed the sheer thrill this brings me, how much our audience encourages me to fuck Seph to the best of my ability. But after hiding, it feels good to be so open about it. To let everyone know how I am hers and she is mine.

As Charon ushers the last shade off his ferry, he says, "You've one soul left to judge."

Hades, or what remains of him, stumbles into the room. His once lustrous dark hair and beard are dull, gray streaks peppering through the black. As he speaks, his eyes don't leave where Seph sits on me.

"Your Majesty. You must help me. I've no memory of who I am. No idea why I'm here in this place."

Seph doesn't speak. She only lifts her skirts as she shifts on my lap, granting Hades a better view of how her pussy wraps around my shaft. Raising her hips in the slightest, she makes more of both our cum leak out, then seats herself deeper. My now-soft dick twitches, threatening to revive itself as she speaks with authority.

"You've a lot of nerve coming here." She turns her head, looking at me from over her shoulder. "Seeking a round two, my love?"

"If it pleases you."

Seph answers with action, undulating her hips so she rocks on me. The movement stiffens me further, and she sighs in pleasure as I snake a hand up. I push beneath her robe to cup her breast, rolling her nipple between my thumb and index fingers. Even at my languid pace, the sounds of me thrusting up into her are downright sinful.

In a sight I've never seen, Hades lowers to his knees. He hits the stone floor with a deep thud, but Seph and I don't stop. Not even as he begs for mercy. The whole time, his gaze is trained on my claiming of Seph's cunt. Not once does he meet her eyes, fixated instead on me filling her. Like even though the Lethe stole his memory, some part of him can't let go.

Once we've both cum again, Seph declares, "Shade, I banish you. Enjoy the deepest pits of Tartarus, alongside the ancestors of the gods."

In a puff of smoke and hellfire, Hades is gone forever. After the remnants waft away and we've cleaned ourselves of our mess, Hermes arrives, proclaiming that flowers bloom in Asphodel.

ACKNOWLEDGMENTS

First of all, I'd like to thank you, dear reader! I'm grateful that you decided to try my Greek mythology reimagining a chance. I know there are a lot of folks with their own take on Persephone, so thank you for reading mine.

I've had such a deep love for Greek mythology since I was a child. I ready the *Percy Jackson* series when those books came out, which sparked an autistic hyperfixation that's been on and off over the last few decades (the *Hades* games kept that alive and well). So, thanks is due to Rick Riordan and the Supergiant Games team for that one.

Most importantly, massive thanks to my husband and my best friend. Thank you for bouncing off ideas with me and for encouraging me to write this. The both of you are so critical in my life and I love you very much.

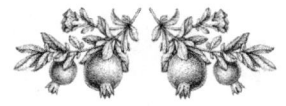

About the Author

ROMANTASY AUTHOR

Lydia Lyre is a fantasy romance author living in the Pacific Northwest. When she isn't writing about gods, monsters, or fae-like creatures taking their clothes off, she enjoys hiking, gaming, and breaking her self-imposed book buying bans at local indie bookstores.